Dreams
That
Drip
MURDER

VICKI KINZIE

Dreams That Drip Murder
Vicki Kinzie

Published by RavenTricks, Longmont, CO

Project Management and Book Design: Davis Creative, LLC / CreativePublishingPartners.com

Publisher's Cataloging-in-Publication
(Provided by Cassidy Cataloguing Services, Inc.).

Names: Kinzie, Vicki, author.

Title: Dreams that drip murder / Vicki Kinzie.

Description: Longmont, CO : RavenTricks, [2023]

Identifiers: ISBN: 979-8-9877205-0-9 (paperback) | 979-8-9877205-1-6 (ebook) | LCCN: 2023901980

Subjects: LCSH: Germans--Crimes against--England--York--Fiction. | Pawnbrokers--England--York-- History--20th century--Fiction. | Murder--Investigation--England--York--Fiction. | Detectives--Mental health--England--Fiction. | World War, 1914-1918--Veterans--England-- Fiction. | Post-traumatic stress disorder--Fiction. | Great Britain. Metropolitan Police Office--Fiction. | LCGFT: Detective and mystery fiction. | Historical fiction. | BISAC: FICTION / Mystery & Detective / Historical. | FICTION / Historical / 20th Century / World War I.

Classification: LCC: PS3611.I669 D74 2023 | DDC: 813/.6--dc23I

Chapter 1

*"No doubt they'll soon get well; the shock and strain
Have caused their stammering, disconnected talk"*

"Survivors"
Siegfried Sassoon
British WWI veteran and poet

(September 26, 1919)

The train lurched forward again. John spied the frayed cuff of his uniform.

Someone during my stay in hospital obviously brushed and cleaned it a bit. Probably Sister Mary.

He remembered his rosy-cheeked, cheerful nurse with the bird-like voice chirping as he boarded the train, "You'll be fine, John. I know it for sure." But Sister Mary was in the past. Tonight, he would relish the smallest details.

As the wheels clacked along the tracks, he devoured the sights, smells, and everything he touched. Each sense left him intoxicated. He was going home. The doctors had done all they could for him and declared him "well enough." Yet he was still unsure. His hands still trembled. Sometimes a lot. The medical staff had made the arrangements for his release, escorted him directly from hospital to the train station, compassionately, and wished him the best of luck, then released him onto this train to Scotland.

Alone.

On many days during his early months of recuperation in hospital, he floated between mundane hospital sights and sounds and raging battlefield scenes. Without warning or reason, his mind sent him back to the intense fighting of a battle he had survived. Long-range guns roared, shaking the earth. Shells crashed nearby, pitching dirt on him. The heart-pounding terror and smell of fear and death clung to him even as his hospital room reappeared, solid and unchanged. The smell of the waxed floors and antiseptic, the sight of his nearby gleaming steel tray, and the soft voices of the nurses in the hallway slowed his heart rate to normal. Such episodes of returning to the battlefield rarely happen now, but enough that he was not totally confident he would succeed. He refused to succumb to his doubts tonight.

No, not tonight, tonight it will be different.

His release from hospital, his journey home—all became intense, exciting and new. The gentle sway of the train, the warmth of the dry September evening. Out his compartment window, the brilliance of the stars, crystal clear in the blackness, watched him ride through the English countryside. Each village awoke in golden light, then drifted past. He imagined the lives, loves, and conflicts of the people in each town. Even the clacking of the wheels or the scream of the brakes as they stopped at each station, the nub of the material on his fingertips as he brushed his hand across the seat, all felt significant and invigorating tonight, and his fears grew smaller with each mile. He felt his future grow closer with every landmark.

Maybe I have a future.

His silence was abruptly shattered by the compartment door opening. His heart skipped a beat. Only a dim glow from a corner nightlight illuminated the car.

The porter edged in followed by a young woman.

Alone with his sensations until now, John hadn't had to deal with any other people.

Calm, he ordered himself.

"There now, this will be fine, madam. Nice and quiet. Middle of the night is a grand time to travel. Fewer people on the train and it bein' a lovely warm autumn evening and all. Shall I switch on the overhead light for you, madam?" the porter said, eyeing John.

She sat opposite him next to the window and shook her head. "No, leave the nightlight on. Then I can watch the countryside pass by."

The porter's lips formed a smile for her. He glanced at John dismissively and left, closing the door to the compartment as quietly as he had spoken to the young woman.

Now there were two of them in the compartment. John held his arms to his sides to disguise the tremor which had started as soon as the door opened, then he studied the cuff of his uniform again. He crossed his legs and uncrossed them and cleared his throat. The dim shadowy light of the compartment, which had wrapped him in calmness, now seemed embarrassingly dark. The young woman sitting across from him appeared to be oblivious to the dark and to him. She sat close to the window staring out, without moving.

Ivory skin, white cotton gloves, brown hair pinned up beneath a black beret, her skirt was a Kennedy tartan plaid, precise dark green and grey squares with thin red and yellow lines. John wondered if she knew she wore a Kennedy tartan and if she was a Scottish lass going home like him. She was the first woman he had been near for a long time who didn't smell of hospital. He inhaled.

She smells just as I remember, like a live woman from before the war smelled.

The war had ended nearly a year ago, but on this, his first day reentering the world, it looked like it had always looked, when a perfectly mundane train ride was nothing special. He wanted to believe in this reality. The horror of his past two years hadn't touched this land, these people, or this train. He had been nearly catatonic when they delivered him from France, and he had never ventured past the hospital grounds until now. He had gone on daily walks around the extensive compound full of patients in various broken states, both physical and mental, but he had taken no trips into town.

A final horrendous act, somehow even worse than all his combined war experiences, had, in the end, closed down his sanity. Various doctors, therapy and drugs had brought him this far, but nothing touched that final outrage. Doctor Vintner had explained that John needed to keep exploring and prodding his memory until he unraveled the mystery. But for now, the doctors, who had plenty of shellshocked patients to work with, had decided he might as well go home to recuperate. They hoped he would get better if he was strong enough. They hoped he would fight for his old life back, but that would only happen if he was home and only if he conquered his flashbacks. The alternative would be a terrifying life only half lived in the present and he would be half forever stuck in his personal hell, reliving battles.

It didn't appear to John that the woman sitting across from him saw the things he saw rushing past. She looked overwhelmingly sad like he had been for so long. She held her thoughts to herself, not saying a word to him.

Perhaps I should speak. 'Nice evening. Traveling far?' Something polite should be said to acknowledge her presence and to appear normal. Maybe if someone enters a compartment at night, nothing is required of normal people.

He couldn't remember. His throat tightened. She didn't seem to notice him or make any attempt to make polite conversation. She made no move to settle in for a nap, read a book, or knit. She stared forlornly out the window.

John's confidence started to crumble. He had hoped to avoid interacting with other people tonight, but it was going to be impossible. He needed to leave for a while. He rose more abruptly than he would have liked, coughed, said, "Um," and left the compartment. Taking a deep breath, he walked to the end of the car and crossed into a second-class seating car. Not a lot of civilians, mostly returning soldiers. More men like himself finally getting out of hospital ten months after the Armistice that ended the bloodiest war in European history. A war which had claimed a quarter of its young men.

A man with a bandage around his head, a spot of yellow forming where the bandage covered his left eye, snored loudly while leaning against the window. A few rows farther back two men, also in uniform, quietly played cards. A cigarette dangled from one of the card player's mouths and when he looked up, smoke drifted into his eye forcing him to squint at John as he passed them. Neither card player had legs past his knees. Another man rested his badly burned, scarred arm on the armrest closest to the aisle and stared into the distance.

"Got a match, Captain?" a soldier addressed John. His uniform's empty left sleeve was pinned up close to where his elbow had once been.

John was unaware of any matches but reached into his left breast pocket and found a small box of them, which he handed to the man.

Sister Mary again, he thought. The mother-hen nurse who had pointed out as he boarded the train, "John Ferguson, I put a fiver and a dandy clean handkerchief right in your pocket and that ought to get you safely home."

The man fumbled a cigarette from a pack in his pocket, got one match from the box John had handed him, closed the lid and struck the match—a neat trick using only his right hand—then handed the box back to John as he blew smoke away from them.

"You still in?" He asked, flicking his hand up and down indicating John's uniform.

John shook his head. "No other clothes to go home in. You?" Embarrassed, he knew a one-armed man would no longer be wanted by the army.

The man registered John's discomfort with a small grin. "Nah. They're done with me. Know of anyone hiring one-armed farmers?"

John shook his head again and walked on down the aisle.

Did anyone truly make it home from the war? Back to love and laughter and friends and family?

John thought briefly of the streets along the river and the old harbor of Ayr and the strong, loving mother anxiously awaiting his train. She would have informed the entire village, and they would all know when he was expected. He pictured her wearing her ludicrous ancient, green felt hat whose shape resembled a fisherman's hat only wanting some lures pinned to it to be perfect. He smiled. He tried not to think about London though.

John entered the pub car and looked around. There were only four other men there at this hour. None had been soldiers, John could tell. Soldiers, you could always tell from anguish in their eyes from their experiences in the war. With the men in the bar, one quick glance, not making eye contact, and then back to drinking. He knew this behavior from the visitors to hospital.

The war had ended. Civilians wanted to get back to their previous lives. The ones who hadn't been in the war, no longer looked at the wounded or even at men still in uniform. They wanted no more stories of bravery or weeping like babies or anything. Enough was enough. They ignored soldiers.

John walked up to the bar. "A pint of bitter, please."

"From up north then, are you?" The barman pulled the ale and set it on the bar.

John formed his face into what he felt must surely be a pleasant affirmative and paid.

"Near Glasgow I'd guess." The barman took the five-pound note and laid down the change.

John nodded his surprise, "Close to it. In Ayr." He had given up trying to lose his Scottish accent a long time ago.

The barman said, "I used to work up there, in a riverfront bar in Glasgow, so I can usually tell. What unit were you with, the Black Watch?"

"The Royal Scot Fusiliers."

"Probably saw a lot of action then, eh, Captain?"

John presented the barman with another pleasant face not wanting to think about the action his unit saw. He picked up his pint of ale. His earlier composure started to evaporate, and his hand began to shake even though he tried to steady it. The barman discreetly looked away. He had served many returning soldiers and knew that noticing their various afflictions only made the men more nervous.

For John, the familiar bitter molasses flavor of the ale brought back pleasant memories of men drinking together. It felt right. It felt like the past before he was a soldier, when he was a civilian with a life. He got a flash of Alistair Howell, his old boss and mentor, and hoped Howell would never see his tremor.

A small balding man, wearing a threadbare tweed suit coat and rumpled grey wool trousers, stepped up next to John and asked for a pint in broken English.

"I ain't servin' no damn Kraut!" The bartender spat the words at the man who recoiled in alarm. The other men turned to see who the bartender was yelling at.

The man turned to the room and protested, "I no German. I Fleming. I refugee." He held his hands out as a shield, as if to stop the bad feelings, his shoulders shrugged a plea for the other men to leave him alone.

A large man with porkchop sideburns and bushy eyebrows sitting at a table stood up and came to tower over the Flemish man. "You sound German. Doesn't that sound like German to you blokes?"

A smaller, younger man rose from his chair, "You best leave, Kraut, or we'll throw you out."

John set his glass down, his ale sloshing around nearly spilling on the bar. He shoved his hand, Napoleon-style, between two buttons on his uniform. He wanted no confrontations and searched for a way to end this. He surprised himself finding it made no difference to him if this man was German. He hated no one. Hatred had reigned too long. Perhaps the man told the truth.

He asked quietly, "Do you have any identification? Any way to prove you are not German?"

The man turned to John, startled at the change in tone. He thought frantically for a moment, fumbled in his pocket, and produced an envelope addressed to "Klaus Van der Buerse."

"That is I. Klaus Van der Buerse. I from Flanders. Is part of Belgium, no Germany." He wagged a finger and spat out the word "Germany" in the same way as the others, as though it was a bad word. He seemed positive this explanation would prove adequate.

But the big bushy-browed man growled, "'Klaus' sure sounds like one of them murdering Kraut names to me."

The others nodded their agreement.

John knew how terrible the war had been for Belgium. Many of the worst battles with the French and British against the Germans were fought on Belgian soil.

He said to no one in particular. "Belgium suffered a terrible toll being in the middle of the conflict. There are thousands of refugees."

"Yeah, and Germany suffered and some of 'em are hidin' out here pretending to be somethin' they ain't. Besides, if he's Belgian, he'd speak French."

John had learned a little about Belgium while fighting there and across the French border. "Only half of Belgium speaks French, the other half speaks Dutch. And, names with 'Van' in them are Dutch and Flemish, not German." He pointed this out as if it were irrefutable, although he really had no idea if any Germans had 'Van' as part of their names or not.

The men stopped and thought about that while Mr. Van der Buerse vigorously nodded his head.

John used this as his excuse to allow everyone's attention to move elsewhere and said to the bar in general and the bartender, "I'd like to buy Mr.

Van der Buerse a drink." He pulled out some more of the money Sister Mary had given him for his trip home.

Each man settled down after that and brooded over his own private memories.

John's success in deflecting a bad situation gave him a bit of confidence. After a couple of drinks, he walked back to his compartment feeling a little more relaxed, hoping the woman had fallen asleep by now. Facing down angry drunk men was one thing, but an inscrutable, beautiful woman was another and more of a challenge than he believed he could handle.

When he entered the compartment, she was still staring into the black void of the darkened window. He felt emboldened by his encounters and his composure this past hour and decided to speak to her. He hadn't fallen apart or made a whimpering fool of himself since his trip back to the real world began. So far.

She patted the seat next to her. "Would you mind sitting next to me? I think I might feel less afraid of everything if you did."

As soon as he sat down, she spoke up, startling him. "Don't you think the stars are particularly bright tonight?"

"Um, yes." He looked out at stars permeating the darkness. "I noticed them earlier."

"Sometimes they seem so close to us, they might be eavesdropping on our lives." She smiled briefly and glanced at his face. Then turned back to the window.

"Of course, if they really could do that, they would know what a horror life on earth is." Then he added, "They would probably stop shining on us at all."

She sighed and looked back at him as if he had destroyed an illusion she was creating to convince herself all was not chaos.

John felt ashamed of himself and tried to think of something encouraging to say.

"We always have tomorrow, and it always could be better."

A direct quote from someone at hospital, probably Sister Mary. It sounded like her.

The woman stared directly at him. "No, we don't always have tomorrow. And it won't be any better or even bearable because the sun comes up once again." She inspected his uniform as she spoke as if to say anyone in uniform ought to know that.

He knew the cliché was absurd even as the words came out of his mouth. "Of course not."

"We only have tonight," she went on. "It is the only thing that is real. All of our life before right now is dead—not only our loved ones, everything. No matter how hard you wish, you can't change the bad or relive the best times." Her face brightened a moment as she said the last. She looked out the window again.

John looked at her faint, sad reflection in the glass pretending to watch the stars.

"What are your plans?" he asked. "No past. Only tonight and the future." He couldn't imagine anyone left safe at home in Britain could feel so defeated.

She turned back to him, "I am so worn out, so incredibly weary, I don't have the energy for another day. It would be so peaceful to simply be dead. No more anxiety or terror or sadness. That's all I want. Doesn't that sound wonderful? Those stars out there placidly watching the dead slumber."

Since finding himself safe again in England in hospital, he had felt all emotions, from horror to repulsion to an incapacitating guilt. The thought that he might always live between the half worlds of sanity or locked in illusory combat terrified him. But not until a woman safe from the exploding shells bluntly said she might end it all, did it occur to him that suicide had never crossed his mind. He wanted to be whole again. He ached for life to be back the way it was, and he knew, as terrified as he was, he would fight his demons. He would fight all the demons in hell to regain all that he had lost.

"Be strong and it will get better."

What an excruciatingly inadequate and embarrassingly simple thing to say.

"Life is…" He paused.

Life is what? A flood of images poured forth of men gasping for their last breath, terrified of death. Images fresh from the mental ward. How to describe rotting corpses of young men who dreamed of a future until the machine guns mowed them down. Anyone who survived that had a responsibility to live. I know it, even if I don't quite believe I can do it.

She knew none of that and couldn't see it. No words. She stared at him as if he were a simpleton.

Thoughts and images swirled, but his words had to be forced out.

"Life is good." He started to perspire, then added, "There is the guilt of surviving when you are not the one who deserves it."

That also sounds lame, utterly without power to anyone who doesn't understand such consuming guilt.

Her desolation touched him. He felt an equal desolation in himself. How could he explain that she had to fight that? She needed to fight for her future.

"You must have so much…a beautiful woman…Do you have a husband, children?"

Her face looked pained and she merely turned away from him.

Such a feeble attempt.

It became vital to make her understand. If her world wasn't worth living in, his certainly wasn't.

Out the window numerous tiny lights of individual lives in houses gleamed as the night flew past streaking her image. His answer appeared as if from some god somewhere. He felt calm and sure.

"I agree with you. We really have only tonight. This moment. The incredible beauty and tranquility speeding by outside the window. The slumbering villages and sweet harvest fragrances are as achingly real as anything bad that has happened to you. Revel in that right now and tomorrow you will have tomorrow. And the only way to see what marvelous things happen is to be there. If only you can see it, life really is good."

Tears glistened in her eyes. She turned to him and looked into his eyes. Then she kissed him. Her lips eagerly meeting his.

His hand touched the smooth whiteness of her throat. He watched her close her eyes. She let her head fall back. He tenderly kissed her throat. Then her lips. A soft deep moan escaped her, and he held that sound inside him. Even while she passionately returned his embrace, he knew her embrace was not for him.

John glanced out the window as the train slowed and saw the station sign. "York."

She gathered her things, pushed open the door, hesitated and looked back at him, almost saying something. Then she turned without a word and left.

A moment later she appeared under the station light and stood silent and erect, not looking in his direction. He stood up rashly, thinking about getting off the train and going to her. He wanted to tell her that she had given him confidence and something—he wasn't quite sure what. A caisson bearing a flag-draped coffin wheeled up next to her under the light. She stepped toward it and touched it lightly.

There lay the man she longed for while she kissed me.

He studied her face and knew he would never forget it.

He sat back down as the train lurched and pulled away from York. He had not felt so calm since—he couldn't even remember when—and discovered tears running down his face.

Chapter 2

"Of course they're 'longing to go out again,'"

(Thirteen months later—November 9, 1920
Two days before the second anniversary of the Armistice ending WWI)

John Ferguson sat at his desk in the old, red brick Scotland Yard building staring out the window of the office he now found himself sharing with Dickie Geevor, the second son of Lord Geevor from Cornwall. Rain sheeted down the window. John's mood matched the weather. Dickie hunched over papers, scrutinizing them with uncharacteristic interest. John thought there must be some glory hidden in whatever he was working on or it would never have absorbed Dickie. John had worked with him before the war and always thought Dickie's father must have sent him to London to get him far from home and probably got his son this job at Scotland Yard through someone important who owed the old earl a pretty big favor. John was not alone in his view that Dickie wasn't too bright, and further that his promotions were based on his lineage, not his ability.

John's own lineage included fishermen, crofters, and merchants but not a drop of noble blood. Dickie—in his snobbishness—found it hard to believe that this Scottish peasant had ever been allowed to become a detective, a murder investigator with the Metropolitan Police–Scotland Yard. Dickie's feathers had been further ruffled when the illustrious Detective Chief Inspector Alistair Howell became John's mentor instead of his own. When John left for the army four years ago, Dickie had moved into his place, literally his space, making John's desk his own, and yet Howell had still ignored him as much as possible. Now another desk had been moved in next to Dickie's for Detective Inspector John Ferguson to be welcomed back by Howell.

Dickie nearly always caught desk assignments. He did research and background and filled out reports. It was a safe place to keep him. But John reflected, for the five months since his return, they had both sat at desks out of harm's way.

Alistair Howell had been promoted to superintendent last year, and it was through his influence and reputation that John had been asked to come back to Scotland Yard. His superiors had allowed him in the office, at Howell's insistence, with the hope that he would get up to speed. Unsure of himself, John used every excuse to stay firmly behind his desk, although he detested the whole paperwork aspect of police work.

Dickie was not alone in waiting to pounce on John's errors, nor was he alone in resenting his special treatment. A number of experienced detectives had gone off to war making way for the promotion of others. Many never returned to reclaim their positions. Because of the manpower shortage in police departments caused by the war, women were able to serve as special constables for the first time in history, but since the war ended, they had been discharged and replaced by any available man looking for work. With the peace came the closure of most of the war industries and thousands were jobless. Newly promoted detectives worried that those who did return might force them back to the rank of constable, and they would be back to walking a beat somewhere in London. Medical conditions were often the cause of termination. This was no time to be coddling some addle-brained shellshock victim. And John's future wasn't looking promising. If it wasn't for Howell, he would not have lasted this long.

There had been a number of incidents in the five months he's been back at Scotland Yard that left John wondering if he was going to succeed. The tremors, heart palpitations, and an occasional flashback, given the right pressure, always lurked. And the right pressure could come from nowhere.

While walking down the hallway one morning, two officers burst from an office directly in front of him laughing raucously. John was reduced to a trembling, cowering figure flattened against the wall. Luckily, his colleagues hadn't noticed him and had walked on down the hallway, talking.

John returned to the comfort of his office where he cowered, hoping no one would witness the attacks, the flashbacks—where he prayed to get stronger. And Howell kept prodding him. Soon after John's return, Howell had come looking for someone to investigate the murder of a man fished out of the Thames. The ashen, frightened look on John's face had forced Howell to send Dickie who refused to get near the rotting, swollen corpse, covered in the revolting muck it had been rolling in at low tide. This left a young, ambitious, Irish constable named Patrick Mullins to be assigned to prod the corpse for identification. No wallet was found. Once the body was autopsied, it was determined the man had been killed by a blow to the head with a blunt object. The man was found in Southwark and his clothes were cheap, suggesting he was of low economic means. Dickie lost interest. This was not going to be a high-profile case. However, Constable Mullins tenaciously pursued the case, even on his own time after being ordered off the case and back to his regular duties.

The dismal rain continued and John thought about the first time Mullins knocked on his office door. The lad practically quivered with excitement as he shyly asked for John's help with the Thames River murder. The smart young Irishman with wavy black hair and bright blue eyes had infected John with his enthusiasm.

"You are the famous Detective John Ferguson, aren't you?" he had breathlessly asked John.

John almost answered, "I was," but instead said, "I am John Ferguson."

Actually, he wasn't famous, in spite of Mullins's declarations. Alistair Howell was famous. When John was about Mullins's age, he had relentlessly worked and proven that a prominent doctor had drowned his wife in the bath when others had decided they didn't have enough evidence to charge him and were about to declare her death an accident. That had attracted Howell's attention. He made John his protégé, teaching him how to really see a crime scene, to ferret out clues, and to not believe anyone's story until it was checked out. John had received credit working with and learning from Howell, and he had advanced to detective inspector.

A blazing smile sprang from Mullins. "I know this is impertinent, but I was wondering if I could have your opinion about a case I'm working on."

Although John found Mullins's faith in him unsettling, he looked forward to the young man's visits with his wild theories. His first theory on the body found in the Thames cast the deceased as a spy. John patiently asked him who he might be spying for and why. When Mullins could discover not a ghost of an explanation, he then decided the man had been murdered by a jealous husband. John pointed out that the man was old, fat, poor and, therefore, probably not someone's secret paramour. Fingerprints proved who the man was and where he lived in Southwark. Mullins questioned the man's wife, his ex-wife, his boss, his old boss, his cronies, his ex-cronies, always bringing John the latest facts. John remained planted in his office offering Mullins help and advice from his desk. John checked into the dead man's past and discovered he had been in prison with one of his cronies. This pal's cellmate was a convicted blackmailer.

John knew this was pertinent and he pointed Mullins in that direction. Eventually, Mullins proved that the dead man was involved in extortion with his partner, blackmailing some important people.

John mustered the courage to accompany Mullins to the apartment of the deceased man's partner and instructed him how to thoroughly search, guiding him to discover the hiding place of a stash of money and a distinctive ring. Mullins was proud of discovering these clues, and John was proud he hadn't embarrassed himself. The young man was turning out to be an eager learner, not only sharp but hungry to prove himself and advance beyond the title of constable. John identified the insignia of the ring which belonged to an exclusive men's club and sent Mullins to discover the owner, who was brought to the office for John to question. The man confessed to being blackmailed by the dead man and his partner. Through insights from safely within John's office, he helped Mullins discover evidence that the deceased's partner had killed him as they quarreled over how to divide the money.

It turned out to be an important case. The murderer was found guilty. Mullins, at twenty-one, had shown courage and initiative in solving the case and had been promoted from constable to detective constable, or DC Mullins, as a result. He had rushed in, brimming with pride, and told John about his promotion. John was excited for the young man, but also relieved that he would no longer be the object of so much admiration. The ambitious

Patrick Mullins had important things to do now and took more cases outside of the office. John hadn't seen DC Mullins for a couple of weeks. He grew more restless to escape the office, himself, and to be out on the streets again.

A knock on the door brought him out of his reverie and Dickie said petulantly, "Yes."

A constable stepped inside and said, "Ferguson, Howell wants you in his office immediately."

John nodded and the man closed the door and left him with Dickie's eyes boring into the side of his face. He simply stood up and walked out of the office refusing to acknowledge Dickie's unasked questions. He couldn't have answered anyway. He had no idea why he was being summoned.

Walking upstairs and then down a long hallway with the names of each superintendent painted on opaque half-glass windows, he stopped in front of the one with "Superintendent Howell" painted on it and knocked.

"Come in," the superintendent said impatiently. John stepped into a small office crowded with filing cabinets. A large desk sat in the center strewn with file folders and papers and a black telephone perched on one corner. Howell had never had a telephone downstairs in his detective's office. A sixty-year-old man with a few strands of light brown hair combed across his head, a jolly face and rotund body belied the cunning which had enabled Alistair Howell to solve some of Britain's most gruesome crimes for the last thirty years. And he had taught John all he knew about his job.

Alistair Howell had devoted his life to his career. It was rumored he once had a wife a lifetime ago. John probably knew more about Howell's personal life than anyone, but even he didn't know about Howell as a young man. Since Howell's wife had been erased from his life through death or divorce, no one knew which, he had been regarded as a driven man on the rise. Most of what he did was calculated to advance his career. The harder and more perplexing the case the more appeal it seemed to hold for him. When he solved a case, he relished the fame as well as the power it gave him at the Yard. His colleagues looked upon him with esteem as well as some jealousy while his fame made him a man with powerful friends.

Sir Arthur, the Scotland Yard Director of Criminal Investigations, handled John with care since Howell was one of the best. When Howell succeeded, Sir Arthur looked good. Arthur Newburg had been knighted by the king for his amazing leadership of the Criminal Investigation Division, or CID, of the Metropolitan Police, better known as "Scotland Yard." Sir Arthur was a man driven by ambition, but more importantly for the force, he was driven for Scotland Yard to be the top police force in the world, which in fact it probably was.

Howell saw John's innate abilities and understood his ambition before John himself did. He had groomed John as his partner, thereby increasing the number of solved cases they had together. And John had been a rising young star. But now many questioned why such an ambitious man had brought Ferguson back in such a fragile state. But Howell knew that if Ferguson could overcome his shell shock once and for all he would quickly rise to prominence as a homicide detective which would reflect beneficially on Howell. That, and the fact that he genuinely liked John.

And now, five months after John's return to the Yard, Sir Arthur was demanding results. He had heard from someone of Ferguson's nervous reaction to mild provocation. Howell could picture Little Dickie whispering in Sir Arthur's ear about the fragile detective. But Howell was aware that Ferguson had suffered no apparent ill effect from searching the Thames murder apartment with Patrick Mullins. Howell now had the perfect case for him. It was high profile. John worked well under pressure, and outside pressure did not cause him to lose focus. However, a simple fact remained, if he couldn't solve this case, Howell could no longer support him.

"Ah, Ferguson," Superintendent Howell's annoyed tone changed immediately. "How are you? How are you, my boy? Sit down."

John sank heavily into one of the two chairs facing the superintendent's desk and looked at Howell warily.

Without waiting for a reply Howell said, "Let me get right to it. I have an important murder case, Ferguson, and I need you to attend to it. I need an experienced detective on this one." He glanced at John to see his reaction as he rushed through the information.

John made no comment and stared at his hands. He looked pale to the superintendent and seemed to be too thin. Howell noted that John's thick, sandy-colored hair swept across his forehead in a way quite different from the current slicked-back style popular with young men today. He also retained his bushy mustache adopted by many regiments during the war. But then, Howell reflected that John never did keep up with fashion.

Howell opened a file and began. "Last night there was a heinous murder up north, and they've asked for help from the Yard. For several months, it's been nothing but paperwork for you, I think. But it's time, John, for you to get back to serious detective work."

Howell's tone was upbeat and positive. He would ignore any qualms John might have about taking his first murder case since his return to work.

"I don't think the time is right." John started.

Howell interrupted. "It's time, John. You've been hiding behind your desk too long. This case is important, and I need a good man on it." He handed the file to John and waited.

John's mouth felt too dry to speak. He swallowed and whispered, "I don't believe..." He couldn't think of any excuse that Howell wouldn't see through immediately. He had been allowed to coast, and now the moment he dreaded was here. Howell was right. He had to attempt some real work, even though he knew this case would determine his future as a detective.

"I believe you can do it. You are a good detective, John. You know that."

"I was," he corrected Howell.

"No is not an option any longer. I am getting pressure from Sir Arthur."

The fact that he insisted John be reinstated and had allowed this much time behind a desk was a testament to Howell's belief in his ability, but as always Howell needed to see some results.

John knew Howell's support would evaporate when Sir Arthur lost patience.

"Working at a desk really is not for me anyway. I hope I can."

A brisk knock interrupted them, and the door opened. "Do come in my boy. We were scarcely getting started on this case."

The eager-smiling, scrubbed, young Patrick Mullins stepped into the room and shut the door. Howell cast a disapproving glance at John as he sighed. DC Mullins was about to be assigned to assist him up north on this case, and John was not sure he could do this job or handle Mullins' youthful exuberance and his adulation.

The superintendent asked Patrick Mullins to sit down and repeated the little he had shared with John. It appeared that the wide-eyed young pup with little detective experience and the battered and bruised, possibly irreparably broken, old detective were going to attempt a murder investigation together.

Actually, John wasn't old at all. He was only thirty but compared to Mullins, he felt impossibly older. John's career had been flourishing. Then came the war. He had finally fallen victim to public pressure to join the army when he was twenty-six. He remembered being startled by someone grabbing his arm as he walked down the Victoria Embankment. A hatchet-faced humorless woman asked, "Why are you strolling along here without a care in the world? Do you not know your king and country need you?" she asked self-righteously, her voice rising in volume. "Your freedom is being purchased by many thousands of brave British lads while you cowards walk safely around London." Her strident voice drew the attention of people passing them on the sidewalk. Pulling a large white feather out of her handbag, she thrust it theatrically into his hand and marched triumphantly away, eyes gleaming, having done her part for the war effort. He stood dumbfounded and embarrassed, holding the feather, conscious that everyone who passed him knew its significance. Some women had taken to giving them to any young man not in uniform. These were silly, sanctimonious women, oblivious to the fact that millions were being killed in trenches that turned out to be extraordinarily efficient on both sides for little or no gain. But then he hadn't known the futility of the war at the time. John's service to Scotland Yard, he had thought, was enough, but her feather had bullied him into enlisting.

Superintendent Howell brought him back to the present. "A successful businessman has been murdered, savagely stabbed numerous times in the chest. The chief constable of York has actually requested our assistance in solving this one."

This time a gasp escaped from John's lips.

York. The beautiful, young woman on the train, he thought. The months he spent getting stronger in Scotland, separating flashbacks from reality, and the months hiding at his desk. He remembered the despair on her face. The longing in that kiss. The courage and focus she gave him.

"John, what? Are you still with us?"

"Sorry, sir."

"You know something about York?"

"No, nothing at all. Sorry. Go on." A glance at Mullins's face, which revealed his somber concern, irritated John.

"The thing that concerned the chief constable of York was not a lack of suspects but, in fact, he has too many suspects. It seems this businessman was a pawnbroker and a German immigrant. Maybe the fact that the second anniversary of the Armistice is only a couple days away brought up some bad memories for someone and he blamed this poor German sod for his own pain. Or maybe it was someone who couldn't redeem his pawn with the economy in such a mess."

John put both hands flat on top of the open file as if to emphasize what he was saying. "Nearly two thousand strikes of workers in Britain since the war ended shows the mess the economy is still in, which has forced lots of good working people to pawn valuables to survive. There will be lots of hard feelings especially toward a German pawnbroker. Maybe someone had a personal reason. Who knows? It's going to be difficult to figure out who chose to murder this particular one and why." John ached to prove himself, to prove he should be back at Scotland Yard.

John could feel the adrenalin rise, like it always had before upon hearing the facts and being assigned a new challenging case. The adrenalin was part terror. Yet he knew this was his only chance.

"John, I'm assigning DC Mullins to you and want both of you on the next train to York." Howell looked directly at John, who kept his eyes focused on the window.

Mullins watched him out of the corner of his eye again, which irritated John. He wanted no more of bright-eyed young men who counted on him.

Mullins could hardly contain himself. But he remained seated until John, after a brief pause, rose to leave. Mullins popped up and practically collided with him in his eagerness to follow him out.

Howell sighed inwardly as they left. He knew Ferguson was too valuable a man for Scotland Yard to lose and hoped he could overcome whatever it was that kept him from being the detective he had once been not so long ago. He also knew if Ferguson couldn't do the job in York, there would be no job in Scotland Yard for him when he returned.

Chapter 3

*"These boys with old, scared faces,
learning to walk"*

(November 10, 1920—York Just After Midnight)

John watched from the station platform as the mist whirled and coiled, sucked down the track after the train. Mist banshees, chasing the receding lights of the caboose. It was after midnight and John felt exhausted already, before they had even begun. Even Mullins was finally quiet. His enthusiasm, not to mention his conversation, had lasted through most of their trip. The rain had stopped, but water from the station's eaves, dripping onto the platform boards, reverberated distinctly, rhythmically. The light shone on a gently swaying bright white plank with bold black letters which read "York."

Once, on his way from his home in Ayr, Scotland, to London, he had actually gotten off the train in York looking for her, the woman he met that night on the train from hospital. Her under the sign at the station and the memory of the night on the train nearly engulfed him. Maybe she needed nothing from him, but he could thank her for giving him the courage he needed once he got home. "Be strong and it will get better," he had told her.

The night traveling through York on his way to London, he realized he knew nothing about her, not even a name. He had watched the train pull away without him while the absurdity of finding a woman with no name in a city the size of York sank in. He simply sat down and waited over an hour for the next train to London.

Before his return to Scotland Yard, his mother, fierce in her determination to keep all stress from his life, had managed a stress-free existence for months while he recuperated. At home in Scotland, he relearned a pace of life that didn't require hyper-vigilance. Still when a flashback terrified him or the night terrors came, he kept the memory of the woman from York nearby.

Once again, John stood on the same station platform, where he last saw the woman, this wet dark night, listening to raindrops march off the roof at a rapid pace, a loud cadence ringing in his ears becoming louder. Drips became the boots of men marching, the sound increasing and becoming the rhythmic boom of great cannons and unceasing noise and terror. Abruptly, his world restructured itself and became a cot in the inky blackness of a foxhole. Captain John Ferguson of the Royal Scot Fusiliers gasped, unable to breathe while dirt sifted down on him after each concussion from thousands of bursting shells. Realizing he was holding his breath, expecting any second for the beams holding back the earth above his cot to give way and cave in suffocating him, he scrambled outside in the predawn morning. Shells had to be exploding inside his head. Nothing else could be so loud. He screamed at his men, but they merely looked dazed and terrified. He realized they couldn't obey orders they couldn't hear since even he couldn't hear his orders. The pounding explosions made the ground quiver, suddenly bulge up and drop beneath their feet, heaving and plunging all around them.

Mullins watched John stare at the dripping eaves and knew something was wrong. He had seen him suddenly start to shake and try to hide it when they searched that apartment for the Thames murder together, but he had never seen him stare off, unhearing. DI Dickie Geevor had warned Mullins that all was not well with Ferguson.

"He's quite mad, you know. Wouldn't trust him too far. Only here out of pity, war vet and all. Mark my words, he's on the outs and they will quietly retire him." Geevor had tapped the side of his nose indicating this was a word to the wise.

Mullins thought, *Nuts to that. The inspector is merely tired tonight.* Mullins had read all his old cases and watched alongside Alistair Howell for the old brilliance. Mullins planned to protect Ferguson until he got better and to learn how to be a great detective like him.

Ferguson will get better. He simply has to.

Mullins cleared his throat, rushing John through a vortex landing him, stunned and shaken, back on the York station platform. Mullins walked toward the station door, picking up his bag and a small, black leather murder bag given to them at the Yard before they left.

John blinked, looked around at the dripping dark night, then glanced at Mullins's back silhouetted against the light flowing from the open door. Picking up his own bag, which began to shake with the vibration of his entire body, and walked into the station.

Why did it happen now? If simply being tired could trigger it, what will happen in the next few days?

He swiped at the sweat on his face, but it still ran down the sides as they entered a much too bright and much too warm room. A stocky, uniformed York constable sat across the room, sizing them both up but staring at John. He had watched through a small station window as the inspector froze up on the platform in some kind of trance and then walked in shaking and sweating like a pig. What in the world had Scotland Yard sent them? He decided to hope for the best. As John and Mullins neared him, he stood, took off his hat, and tucked it under one arm. He patted the top of his head a couple of times to flatten the curly thatch of black hair which sprang up at an improbable angle.

"Inspector Ferguson? I'm Constable Kitchen, here to take you to your hotel. The chief would then like to meet with you about eight in the morning if that'd be convenient."

"That would be fine," John managed to say and glanced at DC Mullins who showed no sign of having noticed anything amiss in his behavior a few minutes before.

By the time they reached their hotel, John was calm and normal and exhausted. The efficient and fortunately quiet constable had them checked into their rooms in no time. He refused to worry about his condition or the case until the morning.

Almost immediately he fell into a troubled sleep and dreamt he fell from a tall building. Drifting down with no fear in his dream, he noticed detail while he floated. On the small street far below he watched a smart young couple, dressed in the latest fashion, walk arm in arm up to a sinister looking maître d' who held a white cloth folded crisply over his arm. He welcomed them into his restaurant with a wave of his arm and a hungry evil grin. A bright green and white striped awning shaded the entrance. John wanted to warn them of terrible danger, but no words came out of his mouth. Above his free fall, a shadow caught his attention, and he turned to see a score of young soldiers filling the blue sky falling behind him. Some of them looked resigned to their fate, some were terrified, and some looked merely puzzled as they floated to what John knew was their certain death. One of them was his DC Patrick Mullins, and when he reached out to Mullins, John's arm was clothed in his captain's uniform.

He jolted awake terrified and so desolate that he felt the presence of the psych ward closer than he had since they had released him.

(November 10—Morning)

The morning dawned bright and dry and John gathered his courage as he walked down to breakfast determined to fight for his old skills, his old life back. His pocket watch said seven ten. He replaced it in his vest pocket as he took a quick look around the hotel dining room. Cozy, in keeping with the size of the hotel, only about ten tables with white linen and lace at the windows.

"Would you like to sit over here, please, sir?" asked a serious, shiny-faced girl of about fifteen. She led him to his table, and he ordered tea and toast. When she returned with his tea, she looked over her shoulder a couple of times to make sure no one watched her, then asked in a low voice, "Are you the Scotland Yard detective, come here to find out who killed Mr. Gruber?"

"Yes, I am."

"Well, good riddance to him is what we say. Dirty Kraut living right here big as you please all these years, and loaning poor honest working folk money at…"

"Alice! Quit bothering the man and bring him his toast."

Alice jumped and scurried off, head down, as she passed the large woman glaring at him, before disappearing into the kitchen.

Alice would be mimicking adult opinions, he noted. *Some people perhaps think no German has a right to live in York anymore. The high unemployment rate is making pawn brokers rich. Always a cause for resentment. Or perhaps the man was a bad person and someone had a more personal reason for the murder.*

A couple of minutes later she returned with his toast. "Alice, did you know Mr. Gruber?"

"Course. He always had the pawnshop right down the block."

"And you never liked him?"

"Course not. He was a German and we hate 'em all, don't we?"

The large woman came over. "Go on and do your work, you silly girl," she said.

She crooked one arm onto her waist and looked at John.

He said, "Did you know Mr. Gruber before the war?"

"Course I did."

"What did you think of him?"

"Didn't think nothing about him. Had no need to pawn anything. Still haven't needed to pawn anything but many have, and it's a shame they lose family heirlooms and such."

"But he lived here many years. Did he have family?"

"Course. A wife who died and a son who moved away."

"Did you know his family? Did you like them?"

"Course. Nothing to not like. I've got to get busy now and I'd say you probably do too."

He almost answered 'course' before he was interrupted by Mullins.

"Good morning, Inspector Ferguson," said DC Mullins, smiling as he sat down at John's table watching the back of the retreating woman.

"Good morning, Mullins." Memory of his dream whispered a brief warning, but it whisked away before he could catch the why of the warning.

Alice returned with tea for Mullins and smiled sweetly for the young man as she asked him, "Do you also wish some toast, sir?"

Constable Kitchen arrived to walk them to the station house as they finished breakfast. Mullins carried the black murder bag. John glanced back to see "The Green Man Hotel" written over the door. He mentally oriented himself as they walked. Howell had taught him to establish a map in his head to pin pertinent information on as a case progressed. One never knew what might be important. He spotted on his right, across the end of the street, a bit of the medieval, Old Town wall with its notched, crenelated top. Beyond the wall he saw the minster towers jutting up. They walked this brisk morning in the opposite direction of Old Town, straight up Holgate Street on the south side. He observed a familiar well-worn, relatively prosperous street of small merchants' shops. The smell of cigars as they passed a cigar shop, next a bookstore. Across the street was a chemist shop, still closed and dark this early, and the butcher who was setting his sign out front. Most owned by the merchants who ran the shops and who often lived over them.

"Right up here's the pawn shop, where he was murdered." Kitchen said.

Two women stood, heads bent together, staring into the front window of the pawnshop. They backed away from the window as the constable and the two men in suits approached, giving them dark looks and whispering behind their hands, then crossing the street before the three men reached the pawnshop. Through the front window, the dark interior looked ominous when one knew that a terrible crime had been committed there only the day before yesterday. Numerous items for sale visible through the window, including a guitar, a tea set, and some tools, seemed forlorn and abandoned. Mullins wondered if buying something from a gruesome murder scene would stimulate the sale of items in the shop or if it would taint the goods inside--make them seem defiled by the violence. The sign painted on the window read "Pawnshop." The traditional three gold balls, symbol of a pawnshop since medieval times, were painted on the window above the words. Nothing looked disturbed or unusual from the sidewalk.

Kitchen told them, "The murder took place upstairs in Gruber's office." No hint of disturbance could be seen from the street past the shadowed upstairs windows. "Constable Kitchen, did you know the murdered man?" John asked.

A clipped, "No," was the answer.

John felt an undercurrent there.

"What's your theory about the murder?"

That took the young man a little by surprise and he shrugged. He hadn't expected to be asked his opinion, and John could tell the young man wasn't sure his opinion would be appreciated.

"You know this neighborhood, Kitchen. What happened here?"

"Sir, there's bad feelings about Gruber having money when so many is bad off right now and him being a Kraut, I mean a German." He said the word as if it left a bad taste in his mouth. "I figure there were plenty around here would be glad to take back their valuables, you know, and, well, he got the brunt of their frustration. People think he deserved what he got, and they're not too keen on whether you punish the person who done this."

Kitchen then looked from Ferguson to Mullins to see if his remarks were going to be considered inappropriate.

John pretended to be interested in the shop window and asked casually, "Do you think it was justified then, this killing?"

Constable Kitchen turned scarlet red. "Course not! We need to nick the bastard and show him the power of the law!"

John turned to look at him. Kitchen stammered, "And…and you're here to see we get that done. Let's go, sir. We got to meet up with the Chief Constable."

Next to the pawnshop was a pub on the corner. "The Swan" was painted on the wooden sign hanging above the door and written either side of a beautiful white swan placidly swimming on a pond. A man sweeping off the front steps glared at them as they approached. Kitchen glared back but kept walking. After they passed, Kitchen said, "That's Joseph Parker. He owns the Swan. He won't be happy to see us. He's not too fond of police officers. We've pulled in Will too many times for petty stuff, mischief, and even suspected burglary.

"His son, Will, found the murder weapon, a large butcher knife, in the alley behind the pub."

"Do you think the son had something to do with it?" John asked.

"Who knows? Maybe he moved up to breaking into the pawnshop. Mr. Innocent, finding the knife and all." Kitchen shrugged. His attitude suggested he did believe the son might be involved.

As they crossed Mulberry Street, Kitchen pointed out St. Mary's, the area hospital, on the diagonal corner from the pub. It was a large stone Victorian building with turrets on the corners and heavy, stone archways leading to the entrances. "The body is in the morgue in the basement of St. Mary's, but first I'm to take you to the station," Kitchen told them.

They arrived at the station another half block up Holgate, and before they entered, John glanced back down the street. They had been deposited in a hotel half a block from where the murder took place and only a block and a half from the police station.

As they entered, the desk sergeant, perched behind his desk, ignored Kitchen's nod and stared stone-faced at them. No one waited in the chairs across from the desk sergeant and their steps echoed on the marble floor as he watched them pass.

A large man, over six feet tall with a barrel chest, ruddy complexion and thinning brown hair strode towards them. He had once been a powerful man but now, in his sixties, was turning to fat. He stepped towards them and as they shook hands he said, "Ferguson from the Yard? I'm the Chief Constable Harry Weems. And this is..."

"DC Patrick Mullins," John told him.

The chief constable shook Mullins's hand, and they walked to the back of the station into Weems' office. In John's experience most such offices were about as cluttered as this one. Papers littered the battered desk. Several filing cabinets encircled the room, and several framed certificates hung on the wall. Two straight-backed chairs faced the chief's desk. Weems asked them to sit and then ordered Kitchen to retrieve the murder weapon from the holding room. Kitchen immediately slipped out.

"I called Scotland Yard yesterday morning, first thing. Usually, I would fight having a case taken over by you lot. We're not totally incompetent twits here. We solve most of the murders round here." He hesitated a second. "We never have this kind of brutal murder. Our murders are mostly something between people that know one another. I'm afraid this one might affect the whole community. If this is about someone who owed the pawnbroker money, it might give ideas to someone else in trouble right now, and it might lead to another murder. On the other hand, this might be a hate crime since the murdered man was German. And if it isn't solved, York has other German immigrants who might be in danger. I wish this whole Armistice celebration was over, and we could stop dredging up bad memories."

John wholeheartedly agreed with that sentiment. So much attention concentrated on creating a tomb for some unknown casualty of a war so fresh in memory appeared to be prying open festering wounds. Few acknowledged it, yet the atmosphere seemed different. London appeared gripped by the preparations around Westminster, and the newspapers focused on the events. Even officers at the Yard seemed more introspective in their day-to-day activities. John believed the charged atmosphere certainly could have led a person to this murder.

"And," Weems continued, "I don't want this investigation mucked up due to any lack of experience with such a crime. So you will get our full cooperation. But I better be kept informed."

John nodded politely. They both knew Scotland Yard would have appropriated this case. It was brutal. It didn't fit the usual local crime situation, and it would attract national attention—and remain in the public's consciousness if it wasn't solved. But he let the man take credit for allowing them to take command. Maybe he would be more cooperative.

John said, "You seem to be omitting the possibility that the murder was solely personal. Who hated the man? What do you know about him? About his family, his friends, maybe any personal enemies?"

Weems shrugged, nodded and said, "Maybe. Actually, I hope you're right."

"Tell us what you know about him."

Weems recounted the facts as he looked through the few papers in the file, although he hardly needed any notes on the case. "Hans Gruber was sixty-two, a respected businessman, a pawnbroker who had done well for himself. It is a fact that he was a German immigrant, but he had lived in York since he was eighteen. His wife died about, oh, let's see, five, six years ago. I've known Hans since we were young men, and no one had any complaints with him until the war. The longer the war lasted the angrier people got. Then in the last two years since the bloody damned war ended, we've had men coming home needing jobs and decent wages. Not enough good jobs without the war industries. It hasn't been easy for people. Men throughout Britain striking for decent wages. Being a pawnbroker was a lucrative business to be in right now. People always hate the pawnbroker if whatever is pawned can't be redeemed and then they remembered Hans was German and resented having to pawn things to him. Hans never lost that accent of his in all these years.

"He and his wife Fiona opened the pawnshop right here on Holgate Street almost thirty years ago. When they got enough money they moved into a nice house, but he wasn't interested in it after Fiona died, and he had moved back in over his shop."

The Chief Constable's voice kind of trailed off as if remembering an old friend, John thought.

"Did you personally know the victim, Chief?"

Weems sighed, nodded. "Hans and I were mates before either of us was married. We hadn't been close for some years, but he was a decent man." Then he added, "In my opinion. But you never really know about a person." He gave Ferguson a policeman's knowing look. Policemen found and exposed people's secrets.

"Who might know of someone who was close to him recently?" John asked.

"Possibly his housekeeper." Weems looked in the folder for her name. "Estelle Llewelyn can probably help you with more information there.

"Did she find the body?"

"No, a young man from next door named Will Parker found the body." He spat out the name as it was distasteful, like the way people said the word "German."

"I have to tell you, though, his pawnshop isn't a mess. A couple of shelves were overturned close to the back entry. People didn't tramp through the crime scene. Although the murder weapon was handled. I ordered the pawnshop locked up. Here are the notes on everything we've done. I'm loaning Constable Kitchen to you. He can help you with the preliminary information."

John flipped open the file. There were notes from the first constable on the scene and an autopsy report.

Nothing really.

Weems was handing over a crime scene to the Scotland Yard men without much evidence even investigated and apparently little destroyed. John wondered if the young constable being assigned to them, instead of a more senior officer, was an intentional insult. Local police often fought cooperating with the men from Scotland Yard when they lost jurisdiction over a major crime. But this chief constable had requested their help and then washed his hands of something so vital to the people of York. Why? He handed the file to Mullins.

Weems looked at John. "If you require more help don't hesitate to ask for anything you need."

"How much was taken from Gruber's shop?"

"Like it says in the report there, we can't find anything obvious missing. He has shelves of stuff there in the back, and it doesn't look like whoever it was grabbed anything. Gruber kept the place neat and orderly."

John found that amazing. "A bunch of people milling around in there from the pub? People who might have an item on pawn? People in need of money and nothing was touched? That's nothing short of amazing. Did you have an inventory done?"

"Uh, I only sealed the building. Didn't want to disturb anything any further."

"Someone needs to do an inventory immediately. Could you put a couple of men on that?"

"Well, I would need to rearrange some schedules. Shouldn't you do the inventory?"

John found this man's lack of action amazing, almost negligent.

"This could be a break-in that went awry for one item precious to someone. This needs to be completed as quickly as possible. And I need Officer Kitchen to help me investigate more."

"Right. I'll get two men over to the pawnshop within a couple of hours."

John glanced over at Mullins who only looked back at him with a puzzled expression.

"DC Mullins, please note that."

Mullins grabbed a small notebook and pencil from his pocket and began writing. "Two men." Thought a moment then added, "inventory." He looked for a clock, found none and wrote, "soon."

"We have the murder weapon, found by a young man in the alley next to Gruber's back door. He's the one found the body. Created quite a ruckus, he did. Always a wild kid. We've had him in here for theft before and being drunk and disorderly. The lad's only maybe twenty. Ran back into his dad's pub screaming about a body, and people stampeded out of there over to Gruber's. See something ghastly to perk up their evening. Luckily someone ran and found a constable. Once he got there, people had already been in

Gruber's shop, craning their necks up the steps, and a few had even ventured upstairs. The constable found them all back at the pub. There was screaming and crying. A bit of excitement for the pub crowd. It'll be a wonder if anything useful remains from the crime scene. Doctor Berry is holding the body for us right down the street at St. Mary's for you to see."

Constable Kitchen had returned and stepped forward holding out a wooden-handled butcher knife with a ten-inch blade.

"Could I see the murder weapon?" John asked after noting that it had been wiped clean but still had some dried blood on it near the handle. The steel blade had the word "Sheffield" written in small script letters near the handle.

"Any fingerprints?"

"Nothing anymore," Kitchen replied indignantly. "Will Parker said he found the knife beside some rubbish bins in the alley behind their pub. He picked it up like a bloody fool and ran it right over to us like he was too stupid or drunk to know about fingerprints. He's been arrested and finger-printed in the past, so there's no chance he didn't know about fingerprints."

"What makes you sure it is the murder weapon? Maybe this is simply a knife that was thrown away. It was found near the rubbish bins, correct?"

"Uh, it's a perfectly good knife. Why would anyone throw away a good knife? It was found next door to where the murder happened, and it has blood on it?" Kitchen answered.

"Then perhaps we ought to take it with us and see what the doctor can tell us. Does the doctor know what to look for? We brought a murder bag with us."

The Yard had recently started providing a bag full of the latest in gath-ering evidence from a murder scene. They could match a fingerprint found at a crime scene with a suspect's by comparing the two with a magnifying glass. If a gun was used, they could have the bullets microscopically matched.

"Dr. Berry does autopsies from time to time. He has testified for us against defendants before. I told him you would want to view the body first thing this morning so he should be ready for you.

"You have the file and Constable Kitchen with you. I want to be kept informed of the progress on the case," Weems said. "Ferguson, we will help you any way we can. Just solve it."

John thanked Chief Constable Weems, and they left the station after Kitchen tucked the knife into the little black leather murder bag. They went back down Holgate half a block and across the street to St. Mary's Hospital.

Kitchen confided, "I'm the one checked for fingerprints. I read all about Dr. Spilsbury instigating the murder bags. How the Yard uses Galton's Detail of matching twelve points for a positive identification." He was trying to impress them with his knowledge about the bags and, actually, had succeeded in impressing John.

Spilsbury was famous for solving crimes using small bits of evidence found at a crime scene. He was instrumental in the fact that all detectives now took the new murder bags with them on investigations. Numerous police departments were still a little dubious about fingerprints, even though Scotland Yard had established the Fingerprint Branch for matching prints. But apparently, York was not dubious or at least not Kitchen.

Kitchen continued, "I sprinkled talcum powder over both sides of the knife. I asked Jones—he's the constable that received the knife from Will Parker. Jones knew not to touch the handle. But there wasn't anything. No one's prints. That crafty Will Parker erased them, I'll bet."

At least Constable Kitchen was trying to use the technology. He had yet to find any prints for them.

Mullins said, "You think he murdered Mr. Gruber?"

"I don't know that I'd go that far. But he's a thief, that's for sure. And he knows to not leave us any prints. Most people wouldn't know that."

The three men entered the great Victorian hospital building. Kitchen threaded their way through the corridors and descended stone steps to the morgue.

John was dreading this inevitable part of his job. Viewing the body. An important test he needed to pass. He had helped Mullins solve the Thames River case, but he hadn't needed to see that body. He had viewed numerous bodies of murder victims before the war and thousands during the war. This would be the first body John would see since the Second Battle of the Somme. Sometime during the retreat from that ferocious German onslaught is when he lost his mind. He was in hospital when the final Allied victory over Germany and her allies occurred. He remembered ordering his men to retreat along with the rest of the British Fifth Army at the Somme and then nothing. He steeled himself for this test.

The stone room secreted beneath the hospital served as the morgue and felt colder with each step down the staircase. His mind, which he had so painstakingly patched together, might snap back to a nether world he in no way wanted to crawl out of again.

Dr. Berry, a small man, wore a black suit that hung on him like it still held the hanger. He stood next to a bulging white sheet, glowing beneath the glaring light, on a wheeled table in the middle of the room. The doctor smirked at the Scotland Yard man who barely glanced at him. John's eyes were fastened on the sheet.

"Well, Scotland Yard is here so now we can relax, the case will be solved in no time." Dr. Berry's long-pointed nose and small close-set eyes gave him the appearance of a weasel. He sneered at them as he stubbed out a cigarette in a glass ashtray.

Kitchen turned red, embarrassed by the doctor's sarcasm, as he introduced them. John barely registered the introduction. The body, under its wrap, looked ominous.

The doctor watched John's rigid stance as he yanked the sheet back. The greenish-grey naked corpse looked shiny, like the underbelly of fish and reeked of formaldehyde. The chest had been stabbed so many times there was, at first glance, only a dark red sunken section. The skin along his neck folded back from two purplish knife wounds looking like grotesque black lips emerging from the body. There was a single stab wound to the abdomen.

John unclenched his fist as his entire body relaxed. This body held no terror for him at all. It opened a box in his memory that had been sealed for a long time. In that box was his professional policeman's familiar autopsy scene. Dead body–old hat. He was keen to take part in the examination.

"Why the formaldehyde? That's unusual," John asked.

"Usually a body is removed from the hospital morgue by the morticians within hours of it being moved down here. When we've had a murdered body, the case is solved pretty quickly. But I thought the formaldehyde might preserve the extent of the stab wounds, and it might take a while to figure out who murdered him. I'm not sure it helped."

John then asked the doctor to turn the body over so he could see the man's back.

Dr. Berry did as he was asked and pushed Gruber's body up on its right side, revealing one wound near his kidneys.

"Doctor, can you tell anything about the angle of that wound?"

Mullins and Kitchen were motioned over to hold the body on its side while the doctor examined the wound.

John said, "It looks to slant upwards. See how the skin is torn above the hole left by the knife?"

The doctor examined the wound and nodded slightly. Stepping back, they lowered the body back onto the table.

"Was the body found on its back or face down?" John asked Kitchen who was holding their folder.

Kitchen skimmed the page written by Jones, the initial officer on the scene, and was surprised to find that he had recorded, "Face up."

Dr. Berry looked puzzled.

John explained, "The first slash of the butcher knife looks to have been in the back. There was only one wound in the back, and he was found on his back. I believe the knife was pulled out as the startled man turned, and he was then probably stabbed in the abdomen as that wound has an upward slant to it also. The chest wounds and the two in the neck look like they were inflicted while the poor man was lying there dying."

Mullins and Kitchen, as well as Dr. Berry, intently inspected the chest wounds as John explained. Dr. Berry was forced to nod, if only slightly, in agreement.

"How many stab wounds in the chest then," Mullins asked.

"It's hard to tell exactly," the doctor admitted. "They overlap. But at least twenty. Would you say, Inspector, that the man who did this hated this German?" The doctor's face had a half smile and angry eyes.

John wondered where his attitude came from. Apparently, he too disliked all Germans, but why antagonize the detectives?

"Dr. Berry, you seem to have a theory for why he died. I would have thought your expertise only extended to how he died?"

"Germans are all alike, you know. Calculating. Merciless."

"Did you know Mr. Gruber?"

"Course I did. Everyone on Holgate Street and for a couple of blocks on either side of here knew him. He got rich off of people's hard times. He also would make bigger loans to those with some kind of collateral, and he got even richer off those."

"It seems, you never liked Mr. Gruber?"

"Never felt one way or the other." The doctor became defensive. "I never pawned anything. I only knew his business was distasteful."

"Tell me, Doctor, do you believe the knife the police have is the same knife that killed this man?" John nodded to Mullins who pulled the knife from the black murder bag.

"Well, we don't have a lot of expensive knives covered in blood found in alleys, Inspector Ferguson."

The smirking again.

When John didn't respond, the doctor took the knife and inserted it carefully into the single wound on the abdomen. "The wounds seem to match. Same depth to the wounds and width as this knife," he grudgingly admitted. Then he mumbled, "Probably the murder weapon."

John agreed, this was most likely the murder weapon, which Dr. Berry gave back after wiping it off. Kitchen placed it back in the murder bag.

"Anything else in your report we need to see concerning the victim?" John asked as he glanced at the one-page autopsy report. It said only what the doctor had shown them. Hans Gruber had indeed died from multiple stab wounds.

"Any bruising or anything to indicate he struggled with his assailant? Could you tell the height of the attacker from the angle of his wounds?"

The doctor shook his head, dubious that a description of the assailant could be conjured up from the victim's wounds. He pulled the sheet back over the body. "No bruises."

"Will you be here at the hospital if we have further questions, Dr. Berry?"

"I'm only in hospital when I have a patient, and I'm certainly not to be found often in the morgue. My surgery is across the street. Kitchen here can show you when you leave, which I hope is now. I've shown you what you need to know about his death—all in the autopsy report—and if you have no more questions, I have work to do."

As they left the hospital, Kitchen mumbled, "I'm sorry the doctor was so rude. I don't know what got into him."

John thought the doctor's rudeness reflected the attitude of the young waitress, Alice, and the cook. Probably, the same reaction as so many throughout Britain, resulting from the savagery of the war. So far only Kitchen seemed interested in getting to the bottom of this case and that was because he liked forensics, finding evidence.

Chapter 4

"They'll soon forget their haunted nights";

(November 10, 1920—Later in the morning)

The bright, sunny November day, although cool, was warming up as they left the hospital. More people walked past them now and more cars and horse drawn wagons hurried up and down the street. Kitchen pointed across Mulberry Street to the first building on the corner. A brass sign was hung near the door, "Dr. William Berry, Surgery."

"That's the doctor's office. He and his wife live upstairs from the surgery. They also have a couple of recovery rooms for some of his patients who need the doc to keep an eye on them without putting them in hospital. A lot of people don't trust hospitals and most can't afford them."

John made note of the doctor's office. "We need to see the murder scene now."

"Certainly, sir," Kitchen said as he led John and Mullins diagonally across the street past the Swan.

"Behind here in the alley is where Will Parker found the murder weapon."

They walked between the back door of the pub and the rubbish bins. He pointed to a spot on the gravel near the bins.

"Will is the pub owner's son. Would you like to talk to him first? He'll likely be working now. Maybe you could figure out why he didn't tell us where he found the knife and why he had to pick it up." Kitchen looked at the spot and shook his head.

"Not yet. First, I need to see Mr. Gruber's shop."

"It's right next door, sir." They walked into the alley as Kitchen explained. "The murderer came in through this back door, we think. It was found open a wee bit, or so says Will Parker, and the front was locked up tight as you please. Anyway, you can see the lock is intact, no sign of forced entry."

"And there is no one guarding the crime scene?"

Kitchen shook his head and produced a key to let them in. They entered the back storage room of Gruber's pawnshop. Kitchen turned on the light. Rows of shelves held articles waiting to be redeemed by their owners or displayed up front for sale if no one came back to claim them.

John, Mullins, and Kitchen looked around and found that, indeed, nothing looked to be out of place or missing. Only one of the standing shelves had been knocked over. John tried to picture excited, intoxicated people shoving each other, trying to see something grisly and not disturbing a single thing.

"And no one grabbed anything valuable in their mad retreat? I guess we'll know for sure once Weems's men finally do that inventory."

John stepped through to the front of the shop that he spied through a curtain. Nothing seemed out of place. No vacant spots on shelves implying a missing object. It looked to be an orderly shop closed up for the night. The glass display case, usually allocated for the most valuable articles, lay empty, but that was to be expected. It would have been locked away in a safe somewhere. Nothing in the closed unlocked cash drawer.

"Do you know where Mr. Gruber stored valuables at night?"

"It's upstairs in his office. It's a small safe."

The constable pointed the way up the stairs, which were against the far wall. "The murder took place upstairs in his residence. The light switch is at the top."

John led up into the dark. As he reached the top, a shadow caught the corner of his eye. He turned in time to see a rolling pin come at his head. He deflected it with his right arm and grabbed the wrist with his left hand. A woman's wrist. She continued to struggle as Kitchen rushed up behind John and switched on the light.

She screamed, "This is Mr. Gruber's. Get out, all of you. You have no right to be here! No right at all."

"Mrs. Llewelyn! You're not supposed to be in here," shouted Kitchen. "We've told you that. This is a crime scene. And what the devil are you doing up here in the dark anyway?"

"You scared the life outta me when you came in downstairs. I didn't know who you were. Maybe the murderer returning. I'm here to clean up this place. I'm not letting it look like this. It's a disgrace. What would poor Hans—Mr. Gruber think of me?"

John let go of her arm and in a quiet, firm voice said, "Mrs. Llewelyn, please sit down.

She did as she was told.

"How did you get in here?"

Still attractive for being in her fifties, even distraught and uncombed. "I used my key then, didn't I?" She looked at him like he must not be too bright.

Between clenched teeth, John said to the two men as he straightened up, "She got in with her key. She's been cleaning up the crime scene." The volume increased with each word. "No one bothered to put an officer on either the front or the back door or find the housekeeper." Then he focused his attention on the York constable. "Kitchen, did you dust for fingerprints before this woman dusted for dust?" John shouted in his face.

"No, sir."

"Why the bloody hell not? You're keen on fingerprinting, aren't you?"

"We were all told not to touch the scene until you got here, sir."

"Yet no one bothered to protect any evidence until I got here."

"Would you like me to fingerprint now, sir?"

John gritted his teeth and took a deep breath. He was yelling at the one person he had found who seemed remotely interested in finding the murderer in spite of Chief Constable Weems' ineptitude. He took a deep breath and turned to Mrs. Llewelyn.

"No more cleaning. Before you leave—and leave the key—I want to ask you some questions about Mr. Gruber."

She looked at him suspiciously.

"Maybe you could help us find out who did this terrible thing. Now then, you were Mr. Gruber's housekeeper, weren't you?"

She nodded, wide-eyed, afraid John was about to yell at her. She plopped down in the nearest chair and began to weep. Perhaps he had finally found someone who cared about the murdered man.

John looked around at a pleasant-sized sitting room while she calmed down. A red Persian rug adorned most of the floor. Red plush couches and chairs with mahogany side tables covered with all manner of things, including an ebony bust, brass animals, silver candlesticks and numerous art prints in ornate carved wooden frames. Silk fringed scarves draped the stands and one adorned an upright piano set against the wall leading into the kitchen. Between it and the far door was an oak table covered with a lace tablecloth.

"Do you know, Mrs. Llewelyn, how long Mr. Gruber lived here above the shop?"

Mrs. Llewelyn stopped crying. "He moved back in after his wife died, and that's when I started working for him. He was a good man. The people around here decided they hated him as the war dragged on, you know. They started being cold to him like he had anything to do with…any of that. It wasn't his doing. He dealt fairly with people. Anyone can tell you that." She looked from one to another daring them to contradict her.

Glancing at Ferguson, Mullins took out his notebook. "When did you start working for Mr. Gruber?" he asked.

"Oh, 'bout five years it's been. He and Fiona had a fine house, but since her death he had no need for a big old house and he moved back. I've cleaned the place, and three nights a week I cooked for him."

"Did you live here, also, Mrs. Llewelyn?" John asked.

"Oh, no, I live with my son. We have a shop across the street."

She nodded toward Kitchen and he nodded back confirming her residence. Mullins duly noted this in his notebook.

John asked, "What time did you leave on the night Mr. Gruber was murdered?"

"Near seven. I made his supper for him, then went home and had supper with my son."

"What was Mr. Gruber doing when you left?"

"He was still in the shop. He doesn't close up until eight usually."

"Do you know if he was expecting company?"

She said indignantly, "What do you mean by that?" Her tone made him believe she assumed he meant a woman, and she resented his implication.

"Maybe a business associate, someone he played chess with every Wednesday, an old friend?"

"Oh," she calmed down. "No one. He rarely had guests. Liked his privacy. After he finished his business in the office, he ate his dinner, read a little, and went to bed."

"No lady friend, then?"

"None," she said flatly.

John wondered if there had been something between Gruber and her.

"If you always left before he finished work, how do you know so much about his nightly routine?"

"I just do." She was agitated. "Maybe sometimes I stayed later—if he asked me to—if he needed something."

"Like some late-night cleaning or cooking." He said it deadpan, and she eyed him to see if he was implying anything.

"Yeah, like cooking."

"And the night Mr. Gruber was murdered, what did you do after you left here?"

"I had dinner with Owen—with my son, Owen."

"Did you go anywhere after dinner?"

Mrs. Llewelyn was becoming more indignant. "No, I did not. You can ask him. He'll tell you."

"Yes, we will ask him."

John looked at Mullins and indicated his notebook. "Interview Owen Llewelyn."

She raised her chin. "Go ahead. I have nothing to hide from you."

John looked around. "Could you show us the rest of the apartment?"

Her face clouded as she looked toward the first room at the top of the stairs which faced the street. John knew that must be the office where the murder had taken place. He allowed her to show them the rest of the apartment first so that he might discern more about how the victim lived before seeing where and how he died. He would wait to see the murder scene.

She stood and led them into the kitchen which was obviously her pride and joy. The kitchen was spotless and modern with a new stove, a gleaming brass tea kettle and pots hanging from the ceiling on hooks. Hot and cold running water in the sparkling porcelain sink. The linoleum was waxed to a shine.

Next, she showed them a bathroom with a hot water tank for the claw-foot porcelain tub and a toilet and sink. Then she showed them the bedroom with a small window facing the alley. It held a bed, a night stand, bureau and a straight-backed chair. John walked around opening drawers. Mullins opened the closet door. Opening boxes produced a pair of dress shoes, shined to a gloss, and a fedora in grey wool. John found nothing stamped with the man's personality—no books or keepsakes, not even photographs of the dead wife or the son.

John compared his own flat. He had secrets. He didn't want people to know he feared he might always be weak and broken, yet he had books and photos of Ayre and the Highlands, letters from his mother and old friends from home, a fishing pole and reel sat in a corner of his closet. Gruber's apartment held none of those things.

These rooms could tell John no more, and he was ready to see the room where the murder had taken place.

"That leaves only the office, the murder room," John looked at Mrs. Llewelyn who showed no inclination to lead them in there.

They left her in the living room. Kitchen stepped through the office doorway and turned on the light.

John held back behind to ask Mrs. Llewelyn another question. "Did Mr. Gruber's customers come up here to his office to make payments or anything?"

"Oh, no. Hardly ever. They did their business down in the shop. Mr. Gruber did his paperwork up here in the evenings."

John turned and stepped into the room. A big oak desk sat in the center of the floor facing the window. Arcs of dried blood had been splashed across the west wall and dripped down a painting of a ship at sea in a storm—now a stormy sea of blood. More blood was splashed across the front wall and drapes. A few drops had run down the window overlooking the street. Blood pooled on the papers on the desk and ran down the drawers.

The scene made John dizzy. The smell. The blood. Death. In the back of his mind, rushing towards him, he heard the screams of men being slaughtered or begging to die, in no-man's land, between the trenches dug into the fields where no one could rescue them. Some of the tortured cries spoken were in German. Unbearable pain sounded the same in any language, especially at night. The roar of the huge cannons. Big Bertha, the ungodly German cannon with a range of seventy-five miles. His heart raced as he fought to keep the screams of the dying and the explosions away.

This is now. Focus. Concentrate.

He grabbed the back of the chair to ground him to reality. He swallowed several times.

I investigate murder, he told himself. *I do this now or I go back to Scotland and die.*

He fought his way back. Trembling and pale, he turned to see Mullins and Kitchen focused on the blood on the wall.

Did they see? Or are they pretending not to notice?

They did see. Mullins was embarrassed by Ferguson's shaking and rigid trance, upset that Kitchen would recognize that something was wrong and not understand everything—or anything. Kitchen's face reflected revulsion and fear, which angered Mullins.

Alarmed at the sight of Scotland Yard's man having some sort of fit, Kitchen wondered, *Is he sick? Does Ferguson need a doctor?* He looked at Mullins. *What should we do?*

Mullins glared at him.

"You can tell Gruber sat at his desk working when he was surprised." Mullins pointed to the wall and followed an arc of blood back to the desk chair.

The words brought John back into the present, and he stepped back from the desk chair. He had succeeded in pulling himself back.

"What did you say?"

Mullins looked around at John as if nothing had happened. "I said it looks like he sat right here at his desk." He indicated the blood streaking away from that point.

John looked closely at it, indicating the angle of the blood spatter and Gruber's position at his desk with his back to the doorway. "No. He wasn't seated. Gruber stood here but facing away from his attacker. Remember, the wound in his back."

"That's right! He would have needed to be standing." Kitchen stood behind the desk chair and made stabbing motions in the air which would have thrown blood exactly as it arced across the walls.

"He probably knew whoever did this. He trusted the man enough to turn his back on him." John touched one of the blood-soaked papers on the desk, his shaking fingertips rattling the papers as he did so.

"We need to look at these papers. Maybe he had taken them out regarding whoever he had allowed into his office after hours."

John then looked through the desk for any clues as to who might have wanted Gruber dead. "Who owed him money? And did he owe money to anyone? Did he keep any secrets in his desk."

Mullins scuffed along the hardwood. "The blood ends abruptly at the floor as if a rug had been here."

"Mrs. Llewelyn! You moved the carpet!" Kitchen glared as if he would like to use his nightstick on the woman.

Only silence from the other room.

"It's rolled up over here next to the wall," Mullins pointed out. "Should we unroll it, Inspector?"

"Yes, but we'll have to move the desk against the front wall."

The three of them moved the heavy desk, and as they did so, a cloth smeared in dried blood fell from the bottom of the desk. John bent to pick it up.

"Look, you can see where the rag got stuck to this leg." A clean spot with no blood appeared on the leg of the desk. "This smells like what? Ether."

He handed the cloth to Mullins who smelled it and then gave it to Kitchen.

"It looks like a woman's handkerchief. Do you think a woman could have possibly done this? Surprised him, used the ether and killed him?" Kitchen asked.

"Maybe two people were involved," Mullins said. "Maybe the woman used the ether and the man did the stabbing."

"Or maybe a man borrowed a woman's handkerchief," John said.

"Why didn't we smell ether on the body?" Mullins wanted to know.

"We didn't smell it because of all the preserving fluids and the morgue smells, but Dr. Berry would have smelled it on the body, and the question is why didn't he tell us about it?"

"Constable Kitchen, would you check in our file here and see if the doctor reported ether on the dead man?" John felt pretty sure that the short autopsy report contained nothing about ether.

"Nothing, sir. It says only what he told us. Why would he not mention that?"

"I think we'll need to ask him that very question a little later. Now let's unroll this carpet.

"Mrs. Llewelyn," he called out to the other room. "Did you move this desk and roll up this carpet by yourself?"

"Course I did. What do you think?"

John felt lucky this strong woman hadn't whacked him with her rolling pin.

The carpet had been, until night before last, a beautifully woven carpet, predominantly red, similar to the one in Gruber's parlor. The concentrated-blood odor that filled the room came from the rolled-up rug, but it provided no information other than the extent of blood loss from the man's wounds. They rolled the carpet back up and placed it against the wall where Mrs. Llewelyn had laid it since it created a relatively clean floor for them to walk on. A squat little black safe sat in a corner under the window.

"Do we have a combination for the safe?" John asked.

Kitchen opened their folder. "It says they found it open and empty."

Then he yelled into the other room, "Mrs. Llewelyn, do you know where we could find the combination?"

In a small voice from the other room she replied, "It's written on the side of the bottom left drawer."

They all looked at one another wondering why and how the cleaning woman knew that, but not at all surprised that she did.

Kitchen read off the numbers to Mullins who opened the safe only to, indeed, find it empty.

John called out to her, stunning Kitchen and Mullins with his sternness. "Mrs. Llewelyn, in here now." Sheepishly, she appeared in the doorway. "Did you wipe any of the surfaces in this room?"

She looked down and shook her head no. "I hadn't got to it yet. I closed the safe and rolled the carpet to scrub the floors, but I couldn't stand being in here anymore and left."

"Well, you may have destroyed more evidence by your illegal presence here than all the people from the pub who entered downstairs but never came upstairs. I may yet arrest you for that. Right now give Constable Kitchen any keys you have to Mr. Gruber's apartment and shop and do not come back in here. Do you understand me?"

Kitchen returned with the keys from letting her out the front door. "I asked her if she had seen anything missing from the shelves, and she said she never had anything to do with the shop. She also stated that he didn't have any assistants. He was the sole proprietor of the store."

Pleased to see Mullins write this in his notebook without prompting, John turned his attention to Kitchen.

"I need you to fingerprint the apartment, the stairway, and the shelves downstairs, Kitchen. We will get the names of each person from the pub who came in here and match prints. Then we can question each one." He turned to Mullins. "DC Mullins, you will examine Mr. Gruber's papers starting with what he was looking at right before he was murdered. We are especially interested in the larger loans Dr. Berry told us Gruber occasionally made. We will also talk to those people.

"But before you do that, I think we should go next door to The Swan and question the young man who found the body and the murder weapon, then you'll come back and check through his papers."

They walked up the alley to the back door of The Swan. As they neared a boy about thirteen bounded out the door holding a huge bowl of peelings for the trash. Kitchen held the door until John and Mullins entered and the door slammed shut behind them. The boy knocked and Kitchen opened it for the boy.

"Eh, thanks. I wasn't fast enough. Damn door is always locking me out," he mumbled as he sped past them and dropped the bowl on a counter, then ducked up the stairs.

They stood in the kitchen area of the pub. A man, a cigarette hanging from his mouth, his shirt sleeves rolled up, slouched over the end of a big table talking to a plump, apple-cheeked young woman while she chopped up meat. She smiled at his story. He seemed to be more leering than smiling as he talked to her.

The man turned to the detectives when he heard them come in. "Officer Kitchen, gentlemen, what can I do for you?"

Each of the policemen checked out the woman's knife and made a mental note that it didn't resemble the murder weapon.

"This is Inspector Ferguson and DC Mullins of Scotland Yard," Kitchen said. "And this is Joseph Parker, the owner of The Swan."

Parker stopped slouching on the table, stood up, put out his cigarette, and shook their hands. "We heard that Scotland Yard was being called in. We hope you can solve this murder. If there's a loony going around killing honest merchants to steal their money, we all need to be worried."

John felt the man wasn't really concerned that robbers would be swarming over the neighborhood, but certainly wasn't saddened by the loss of Hans Gruber.

"Do you believe Mr. Gruber was murdered during a robbery?" John asked.

"Honestly, from what I've heard, it seems to me he was probably killed for other reasons," Parker replied, before turning the question back on John. "Was much taken from the pawnshop?"

John looked around the tidy kitchen as he spoke. The woman kept chopping meat, but concentrated on their conversation.

"Did you get a look at the murder weapon at all, Mr. Parker?"

"Yeah, I did. Will brought it to me, and I sent him to the coppers with it. We're good citizens."

"Did you recognize the knife?"

"What do you mean? If you mean did the knife belong to us, then no, it did not."

"Can I have a look at your knives?"

"Sure." He turned to the woman chopping meat. "Mary, show these men our knives."

She walked over and pulled out a drawer to expose about ten knives of various brands and sizes, none were a match to the murder weapon.

John peered into the drawer and nodded. She pushed the drawer shut with her hip and looked up with satisfaction.

"Mary, did you see the murder weapon? The one found right back there?" John pointed out to the alley.

"No, sir. I ain't around here near that late. I only come in to cook and I'm safe home by six o'clock."

"Thank you, Mary."

He turned back to the pub owner. "Mr. Parker, did you and Gruber get along?"

"Hans? Yeah, we did fine. No complaints. He had his lunch in here for years."

"Even though he was a German? You didn't find it hard being friendly with him while boys from York died by German soldiers? Then he makes money off your neighbors' problems?"

"What? No, no problem. He only ate lunch here."

"Had Mr. Gruber made any loans to you or did you have anything in pawn in his shop?"

Parker smiled a little, "No, not for years. I used to gamble and got in a lot of money trouble—nearly lost the pub. I wised up after that and haven't needed no loans."

"No hard feelings then for Hans Gruber?"

"None at all."

Behind Parker, Mary brought down a cleaver forcefully and hacked off a piece of meat while glaring at John.

"So, Mary," John asked her, "Did you have anything in pawn next door, or had Mr. Gruber made a larger loan to you?"

"No pawn, never with him. He had too much of this neighborhood's money. And no loan neither. What could me and my kids use for collateral? I had a husband, Mr. Detective, who never came home from that stinking war. I don't care if Gruber's dead. I don't care if you don't find the killer. Hurrah. One less German. You should go home and leave it alone."

John could see the reason for all the hostility against them and their investigation. To these people this murder was pay back for all they had endured in the last few years. To the people of York, the death of this German man was justice—not the discovery of the murderer.

John turned his attention back to Joseph Parker.

"We understand that your son found the body and the knife that killed him, and we would like to talk to him if he's around."

"Yeah, he's up front working the bar. You want me to call him back here?"

"Don't bother. We'll go through here and talk to him if he's not too busy."

They walked past the stairwell where the boy had vanished and into the pub. John wanted to see the son at work in the pub before questioning him. The wooden bar was surprisingly beautiful. Polished oak burnished to a golden color, about fifteen feet long with a thick brass foot rail, and backed by a long gilt-frame mirror nearly the length of the bar. Several small tables sat against the walls including two in front of the window next to the door. Three men played a halfhearted game of darts near the rear. They turned briefly.

More hostility, John noted. *To be playing darts and drinking beer at this hour, they must be among York's many unemployed, and quite possibly customers of the deceased pawnbroker.*

A tall, striking young man, apparently Will Parker, stood behind the bar animatedly telling a story to two grinning men drinking a pint. He glanced up and became serious when he recognized Constable Kitchen and realized who must be with him. The two drinkers turned to look, grabbed their glasses, and moved to a table close to the dart players.

"Good morning, gentlemen. You must be here to question me about the murder?" Will Parker's jovial manner switched to serious and sincere. John thought it less than genuine.

Kitchen introduced Will Parker, a lanky youth, who looked to be about the constable's age, stood half a head taller, and was much slimmer than the solidly built Kitchen.

"I am told you found what is believed to be the murder weapon. Is that so?" John asked.

"Yeah, I found a bloody knife right out back."

John glanced at DC Mullins for only a second before Mullins caught on, grabbed his notebook, and started writing.

"How did you come to find that knife?" John asked.

"Well, it lay right there beside the rubbish bins."

"It must have been quite dark. I didn't notice any lights in the alley as we came in and it was late, near closing, wasn't it?"

"Yeah, I think so. The light from the back door of the pub must have shown out, you know, and I saw the bloody thing lying there."

"Really. I noticed that door has a good strong spring on it. It certainly pulled the door quite shut and locked this morning. Did someone go with you to hold open the door?"

"No. I...it...no." He took a breath. "I must have put something there to hold it open. Yeah, I put something in it." He seemed pleased with his answer.

"What, Mr. Parker?"

"What do you mean?"

"What did you put in the door to hold it open?"

"I...I don't remember. Why? Is that important?"

Mullins noticed the men in the corner were now trying to eavesdrop on the questioning. They appeared to be agitated by Will Parker's discomfort. Kitchen glanced at Mullins, recognizing his concern. Individually, both decided to keep an eye on the men. John stayed focused on his questioning.

"How did you come to discover the body of Hans Gruber night before last?"

"Well, I went down the alley, and I noticed his back door open a bit, you know, and I thought I better check. Something was wrong. Near closing and old man Gruber was always fast asleep by eleven. So why would his back door be standing open, you know?"

"And at close to eleven, in an alley with no lights, you decided to walk next door because you somehow saw his door ajar, is that correct, Mr. Parker?"

"Um…yeah. I mean there must have been light shining from the street or something 'cause I saw it." Will's voice raised. He became defensive. He fidgeted with a bar rag.

Mullins caught sight of two men standing up and stepping next to the one holding the darts. Their faces left no doubt they were displeased about the situation.

Will's father stood in the doorway watching.

Kitchen took a step in that direction.

Mullins glanced at Ferguson who seemed not to notice the men in the back.

"Did you find the knife first, Will, or the door ajar?"

"What? Oh, the door first, then the knife. No, the knife first. No, wait. It was the door. Yeah, that's right. It was the door." He looked back to his father. His eyes implored him to come to his defense.

Joseph Parker marched toward the bar. "Look here, Ferguson, what are you saying to him?"

John ignored the advancing father.

"If you found the door ajar, then what had taken you into the alley in the first place? What lured you down that dark alleyway?"

"I…I don't recall right now. I mean…"

Mr. Parker interrupted his son, "Wait a minute. What are you saying? Are you insinuating my Will, here, did something? You think he's lying?"

John knew he was lying, but he wasn't sure whether it had to do with the murder or something else. Weems had told him about Will Parker's petty thievery. He needed to question Will later, alone.

Mullins glared at the six men in the back, working men with rough hands, dressed for work that hadn't materialized this morning. Angry men. Three of them were now standing and had taken a step in the direction of the outsiders in support of their own. Kitchen placed himself between the locals and the Scotland Yard men, trying to stare them down, and wondered if Ferguson had a clue about the situation developing.

"Now look here, Ferguson," the father protested.

"What in the world possessed you to run back into the pub screaming about the body you found, Will?"

Will looked him in the eye for the first time and said in a low voice, "It was truly a terrifying sight." He shuddered and ran his hands up and down his arms in an effort to wipe the whole scene from his memory.

"You know about fingerprints don't you, Will?"

A vague evasive nod. "I wasn't thinking straight. I didn't mean to erase no evidence."

Joseph Parker spoke up in defense of his son, "Since he didn't do nothing, why would he wipe it? It would have proved who killed Gruber."

"But you wiped the knife, Will. Most people wouldn't know to wipe off the prints. If you had nothing to do with this, wiping the prints looks as bad as if you had left your prints on it."

Will Parker nodded without looking at Ferguson.

Will knew more, John was sure, but he would let Will and Joseph Parker worry about it for a while before questioning them again.

"I'll need to finish this interview later at the station. I need both of you to be available. Before we leave, tell my DC, here, the names of people from the pub who followed you back over there." Then in a louder voice, looking around the pub, he asked, "Are any of the men who went back to Hans Gruber's pawnshop in here now?"

Both the Parkers looked over the group and shook their heads. Joseph said, "I don't think so. Will, you see anyone from that night?"

Before he could answer, one of the seated men said in a calm, low voice, "I was here. But I didn't run over there with a group of hysterical fools. If I had, I would'a come out'a there with both hands full of all the stuff I could've scooped up before they drug me away."

His comments got nods and murmurs from the other workingmen.

"And that would have been stealing, Mister…?"

"My name's Oscar Needham. Write that down, boy." He pointed to Mullin's notepad. "Damn Gruber sure didn't need no more money. Filthy Kraut. He should'a been sent back where he come from, not allowed to get rich off Englishmen."

"Kitchen, Mr. Oscar Needham is the first man you will fingerprint." Then John turned to Mullins, "Be sure you get his address, DC Mullins, so we can find him and corroborate his statement." He turned back to the patrons of the pub, "Anyone else have anything to say about Mr. Gruber or the murder?"

The men's eyes dropped and they quieted. Only Mr. Needham's voice could be heard as he murmured his address to Mullins.

"I want no doubt we are going to solve this murder. Anyone who hinders our investigation into this heinous murder will be charged. Good day, gentlemen."

The men stared, unmoved.

John turned and strode out the front door of The Swan, Mullins and Kitchen trotting after him. They stopped and stood in the sunshine on the corner where eyes from the pub couldn't watch, the two young policemen beaming with admiration, which frightened John more than it encouraged him. He was glad when Kitchen spoke up and broke the silence.

"Will Parker is an ass. A lying thief. I enjoyed watching you wipe the grin from his face."

"Well, there is more to Will's story that we need to find out. I'll let him worry about his story for a while and we will question him again tomorrow. But it will be at the station then."

John looked across the street to Dr. Berry's surgery.

"Now, I think I should see if Dr. Berry is at his surgery and ask him a few more questions." He turned back to his constables. "Kitchen, it's time for you to use your fingerprinting expertise. What you need is in the murder bag. Mullins will record everyone's name, address, and whereabouts the night of the murder."

Mullins and Kitchen walked back into The Swan. John crossed the street between traffic to Dr. Berry's surgery.

He first entered a waiting room. An elderly man with a long grey beard, his head bent so low he stared at his lap, sat beside an elderly woman, her grey hair pulled back into a severe bun. A young blond woman with a worried look on her face rocked a baby wrapped in a blanket. All eyes glanced at him as he walked up to the window, behind which sat a stern-looking middle-aged woman with a thin face. She wore a nurse's uniform and frowned at him. A nameplate said "Mrs. Berry."

"Mrs. Berry, I'm Inspector Ferguson from Scotland Yard. Has the doctor come back to the surgery yet from St. Mary's?"

She showed the same animosity as they had seen from her husband earlier at the morgue.

"Yes, he has, but the doctor is quite busy today. Perhaps I could make you an appointment."

A photograph sat on the cabinet behind her desk of a serious-looking young man in uniform.

Maybe the son was killed in the war. Maybe the reason for her and the doctor's animosity.

John began explaining this was police business as the doctor emerged from his examination room to the left of Mrs. Berry's office. Dr. Berry wrote instructions on the label of a brown bottle and explained the dosage to a woman standing next to a boy with sleepy eyes and flushed cheeks from a fever. Dr. Berry recognized John standing there and his expression changed from concern. The smirk returned.

"Ah, Ferguson. Have you come to tell me that you've solved the crime? Who killed the immigrant?"

"Could I speak to you in private, Doctor?"

He glanced at his wife and said, "Of course. In here."

She followed them into the room and stood with her back to the closed door.

John walked over to the dispensary cupboard, with glass front, full of pint and quart bottles, each containing pills or syrup for the various ailments patients might have. Several small, brown glass bottles, similar to the one they had seen the mother take with her, sat on the shelf next to it, above the sink. A box of corks and blank labels sat at the end of one shelf. Little envelopes and matchbox-sized pillboxes lay on the shelf underneath. A long narrow examining table took up the center of the room, and a wall of high windows at the far end provided light and a view of St. Mary's Hospital across the street. A table, with stainless steel medical implements on a white cloth, sat across from the cabinet.

A bright, efficient room for the doctor's work.

Dr. Berry leaned against his sink and looked at John.

"Dr. Berry, can you tell me why there was nothing in your autopsy report about smelling ether on the body?"

The doctor's face clouded for a second before he answered. "It didn't seem important. Someone overpowered and brutally stabbed Gruber. The ether..."

"Is it difficult for anyone other than a doctor to obtain ether? Do you prescribe it to anyone?"

Mrs. Berry stepped forward. Her face, red. Her voice, shrill. "Of course not. We don't have any in the surgery anyway. We would get ether from the chemist if the doctor needed some for an emergency and didn't want to check the patient into hospital. Ask them at the Thornton Chemist Shop right down the street." She looked pleased with herself and looked at her husband for approval.

He didn't approve.

"Really?" John turned back to the dispensary cabinet to read labels. "A surgery doesn't stock ether? I didn't realize that."

"If that's all, I am busy," the doctor said.

"Did you have a son in the war?"

No smirks. No animosity. Only pain from both the doctor and Mrs. Berry.

John knew what was coming next.

The doctor whispered, "Yes. His name was 'Stanley.' Not declared dead immediately. Missing in action at the battle of Aisne. We are assured he is in one of the many graves there." Dr. Berry said with frustration and anger. "So many young men, their bodies were so ripped and maimed that even their fellow soldiers couldn't identify them. Many were buried where they fell."

The doctor spat out hatred and fury mixed together. "Our only son, our only child, a boy of twenty is buried somewhere in France with naught but a small cross that reads 'Unknown.'"

The doctor's fury spent, his body as well as his voice transformed to an abyss of inconsolable sorrow.

"We knew and loved him, our Stanley. Yet, we'll never even get to mourn over his grave."

The doctor put his arm around his wife who sobbed quietly beside him.

Moved, John excused himself. He now understood their anger. He left the surgery past the stares of the growing number of patients in the waiting room, who probably overheard the raised voices. John didn't miss the fact that the doctor hadn't explained why he omitted the ether from his report.

An odd omission even for an untrained medical examiner, unless it was important, and he doesn't want me to know why.

Having finished recording fingerprints and identities of the few men in the pub, the two young policemen were waiting for him on the walkway in front of the doctor's surgery.

"Only Needham admits to being around when Will came in screaming about a murder," Mullins told him as they walked.

"Dr. Berry says ether must be obtained from a pharmacy or a hospital. Mrs. Berry told me I should check with the Thornton Chemist Shop. Do you know where that is, Kitchen?"

"Of course, it's right down the block a couple of shops away—and then I go off duty, sir, if that's all right."

"What are you talking about? I thought Weems assigned you to me for the duration of my investigation—or at least for an entire day," John said as he pulled out his pocket watch. A little past noon.

Kitchen turned bright red. "I...I thought you had been told this is St. Sampson's Day, quite a celebration here. All of these shops will be closing shortly, and people will be going over to Old Town for the fete. Your best bet for questioning folks will be over there."

Kitchen pointed toward the end of Holgate where John had earlier noted the crenelated wall.

"But if you want me to stay, I certainly will. I've never enjoyed policing so much in my life as watching you work a case."

Both the London men looked at Kitchen, puzzled.

"I'm sorry, sir. I thought you had been informed about the goings-on today. There's a big fete. We celebrate St. Sampson's Day. It's an ancient old tradition. Old Town is the walled medieval town and St. Sampson's Square is in the middle. For hundreds of years people have celebrated on this date. There are games, contests, all sorts of things. Some people will be dressed in old costumes. Shops will be closing soon, and everybody will spend the afternoon there—and later, there's a dance. The revelry lasts into the night."

"A murder investigation is our most pressing matter. Mullins and I will process the murder scene with or without you, Kitchen."

"Nearly the whole of York will be in Old Town for the rest of the day. It will be hard to find anyone to question—unless you question them there. Even the chief will be there. Ask him. I'm sure he meant for you to go."

"I certainly will ask him, after I ask the pharmacist about ether. Could you point out the chemist shop before you leave us?

John, Mullins, and Kitchen stopped across from The Swan and Gruber's Pawnshop on Holgate Street, in front of a small shop with "Thornton Chemist Shop" painted on the front window. It almost faced the pawnshop.

Mullins held the door. Kitchen entered first. John watched as Kitchen ran his fingers through his thick mop of hair, which again had no effect on its springiness, and straightened his tunic a bit as they entered. A slender woman on a small stepladder, her back to the men, was replacing a brown bottle of pills on an upper shelf. Watching from a wheelchair near a doorway leading into the back of the shop sat a small, still handsome woman, with keen and curious eyes.

She's maybe fifty. Not old enough to need a wheelchair.

She watched them look around. All manner of potions lined the sidewalls of the small shop. Vitamins, cod liver oil, pain powders and other things in colored glass bottles. Near the front window stood a rack of greeting cards and a bin of fragrant soaps. The room smelled strongly of dried medicinal herbs and flowers, enfolded in little white envelopes with handwritten names and neatly arranged in small wicker baskets on shelves. Behind the counter were medicines labeled "for prescription only." The woman on the ladder stepped down as Kitchen spoke to the older woman.

"Good morning, Mrs. Thornton." He raised his voice as he spoke to her as if she were hard of hearing.

Ruth Thornton's mouth opened a little and she squirmed a bit in her chair, but she made no reply.

"You're looking better each time I see you."

Kitchen turned to John. "She had a stroke recently."

Then he turned to the woman behind the counter. "And this is Anne Winthrop, Mrs. Thornton's daughter."

The woman stepped off the last rung of the ladder and turned toward them. An electrical shock hit John in the chest. The woman who had occupied his mind for the last year smiled at them. A warmth, like melted light, poured into him, returning him to all his feelings on that warm, enchanting night on the train. Her despair and his small bud of hope in a future for her. Her sigh, which had made him ache for so much more from her. She had been there during the raw first hours of his freedom. Her sweet presence and her similar pain when he needed it. It was ridiculous how the brief memory of her aided his recovery—tenuous as his recovery seemed to be. It gave him strength and enabled his return to Scotland Yard. He hoped she had found strength to heal. And she was here. She had chosen life after all.

Kitchen's voice intruded. "Morning, Annie." He turned to John, "She's our chemist now that she's been to school in London and all."

Anne Winthrop looked at them, her eyes lingering on John's face an extra second, but he saw no recognition there.

"Good morning, Tom."

"Tom?"

Apparently, Kitchen has a first name. Funny, I'd never considered Kitchen having a first name until this moment.

Her voice sounded strong and crisp as the November air outside.

"This is Inspector John Ferguson of Scotland Yard and DC Mullins. They've come to find who murdered Mr. Gruber."

The mother, Mrs. Thornton, became agitated but could do little more than open and close her mouth. Her arm raised about three inches. She stared at John trying to convey something to him.

Anne explained, "Mother and Mr. Gruber were friends."

There was something in her voice. Was this an aversion to her mother's relationship with Gruber, perhaps?

"She is interested in you finding out who did this horrible thing."

John was interested in Anne's greenish grey eyes. The color of an angry sea. Her soft brown hair, which he remembered cascading across her neck and shoulders, had now been cut into a fashionable chin-length blunt cut. The first post-war short hair trend he had seen in York.

"Could I ask you some questions, Anne…Mrs. Winthrop?"

"Certainly. Let's step into the back room."

Tom Kitchen seemed eager to follow them, but John excused him to go home.

"No, sir. I'll stay with you. I want to help solve the murder." He said it enthusiastically.

Anne pushed her mother's chair ahead as she stepped through the curtain into the back of the shop.

John stepped in close behind her, trying to breathe her in. He felt calm. No shakes.

He felt buoyant, lighter.

On the other side of the curtain sat a small workroom with herbs and dried flowers hanging upside down from lines, boxes of merchandise, and a table with scissors, tape, string, marking pens and a stool in front. Behind this was a tiny sitting area and the stairs to what he assumed would be the living quarters. Attached to the back wall of the stairs was an electric chair elevator that had been installed for Mrs. Thornton.

Sitting at the kitchen table, a teenage girl pushed her long, almost white blond hair over her shoulder, and laughed at something a little, dark-haired boy said to her.

"This is Lisle, my adopted daughter," Anne said, going over to them and putting her arm around Lisle, who looked up, smiling into Anne's face.

"And this little imp is my son, Edward, who's three." Her voice sounded loving and kind.

"And a half," Lisle added, with a French accent, smiling radiantly. "He's three and a half."

To emphasize the truth of this, the boy concentrated on the three fingers he proudly showed them, held in place by his other hand.

John led Anne away from Eddie to ask questions. Kitchen remained by table-side, eager to stay a little longer and speak to the vision that was Lisle. John understood, then, the need for Kitchen smoothing his hair and tunic as they walked into the shop.

"Do you have some questions, Inspector?" Anne asked.

"Um, yes." He couldn't think of a thing connected to the case to ask Anne. He turned back to Lisle.

"I noticed, Lisle, that you have an accent. Where are you from?"

Everyone, including DC Mullins and Kitchen were puzzled by his first question.

Lisle's smile disappeared, and she looked to Anne for reassurance before answering. Anne nodded.

"I'm from Belgium." Shadows crossed Lisle's face at the memory.

"Lisle lived in Brussels and became orphaned during one of the first battles in 1914 when she was only ten." Anne explained, as she stroked Lisle's hair. "All alone, terrified, and no one to turn to for help. Not knowing who to trust. Thousands of Belgians had been killed and close to a million fled during the war. Many who stayed died of starvation. Can you imagine?"

John could imagine. He had seen too many haunted, orphaned eyes as soldiers marched across mud-soaked fields destroying the land and the crops and taking whatever they wanted, leaving nothing. He had seen children selling everything and wondered what Lisle had sold to stay alive.

"The Red Cross rescued her and brought her to Britain when she was nearly thirteen. Now she is my daughter."

"And Anne is my wonderful mother," Lisle gushed.

"Why don't you take little Eddie upstairs for me?"

The two of them left with Eddie babbling to Lisle, who nodded as if she understood what he said.

"She has been a great help with my son now that I am in charge of the shop, and with my husband and father gone and Mother not able to help." She turned and waited for the inspector's next question.

After a brief pause Mullins blurted out, "Do you sell ether here?"

Anne blinked a couple of times. "No, I don't," she said trying to under-stand. "One would need to get ether from a hospital or a doctor's surgery."

John picked up the questioning now. "Dr. Berry told us that surgeons didn't carry ether, only chemist shops or hospitals."

Anne looked puzzled. "I can't imagine why he said that. No ether at a chemist shop. But why do you need to know? Does it have something to do with Hans' death?" Her face said she was more bewildered than angry about Dr. and Mrs. Berry's statement.

Anne's mother's agitation and squirming started again. She wanted to tell them something.

John stepped next to Mrs. Thornton. "Do you know what she is trying to tell us?"

"No. Mother was his friend." Anne's flat voice said not a friend she liked. "Find out who killed him for her."

"How does she communicate? Can you write, Mrs. Thornton?"

Her eyes were almost desperate to communicate but her head-shaking was more of a tremor than an answer.

"No, she can't. We watch for facial expressions when we ask her something."

"How long had your family known Mr. Gruber?"

"Years. Ever since I can remember." Anne seemed unconcerned about her mother's close friend being hacked to death two days prior.

"Where were you when the murder of Hans Gruber took place?

"Two nights ago? I was here, upstairs at home with my family. That's where I am every night."

John couldn't concentrate. He needed time to adjust to finding this woman. Abruptly, he said, "Thank you, Mrs. Winthrop and Mrs. Thornton." He stared directly into Anne's eyes and knew she didn't remember their mutual experience that had so affected him. "I'm sure I'll have more questions for you later."

They left and Mullins glanced at Kitchen. Mullins thought the initial interrogation brief, but believed the questions had perhaps been a brilliant device to leave them off guard.

"Should I fingerprint them before we move on, sir?" Kitchen asked still holding the murder bag.

John's mind returned to the case.

"Ah, good," he managed. "Do that, then both of you go back to Gruber's and fingerprint every inch of his office. Maybe there is something that did not get destroyed by that housekeeper. We also need her fingerprints. One of you get a set of the deceased's fingerprints, which has also not been provided by the good doctor. And get Dr. Berry's too. We need you to search through Gruber's papers some. We need the names of people who owed him money. I am going back to the hotel and make some notes. Then, I'm going to see Chief Constable Weems and perhaps get some help from some of his men. Surely Weems doesn't shut down the entire police department for this grand party.

He left them at the pharmacy and crossed Holgate, again not noticing the tall square spires of the famous York Minster framed at the end of the street, inside the wall, stoically surveying the old city from its hilltop vantage point as it had done for centuries.

"Good afternoon, Inspector," said the desk clerk at the Green Man Hotel as he entered the small lobby. "I have a couple of phone messages for you." He handed John two slips.

John read them. One said to call Chief Constable Weems and the other said to call Superintendent Howell. John looked up at the desk clerk.

"The telephone is right around the corner there, sir, in that alcove."

In the alcove, a small chair faced a desk with a phone. There was no door to close for privacy, which struck the inspector as odd. A small pad of paper, however, had been provided for the user.

First, he phoned Superintendent Howell explaining that, after viewing the body, he believed rage or hatred of some kind was responsible for the murder. He filled in the few details they had gathered so far and asked Howell if he could find out whether a doctor's office or a chemist shop would carry ether. Howell's anxiety carried through the receiver and made John uneasy. The progress of the case. The progress of John's recovery. Or lack of progress on both counts. Howell withheld his concern, reluctant to press him at this point.

Then he called Weems.

After asking some questions about who John had seen during the morning and what he had learned, Weems said, "There is a fete going on today over in old York. It is a big event here and most places will be closing about now. It will be hard for you to find people around that you might want to talk to, but those people will be over there. It might be beneficial to see them all interacting, which might give us some insight."

John agreed after considering the prospect of seeing the people who knew Gruber interact at a social function. He also agreed as it provided an excuse to see Anne Winthrop again.

Weems told him he would send a car for him and Mullins at three, even though it was an easy walk from their hotel to the Old Town. Weems wanted a police car there as a deterrent for the rowdies who might drink too much later in the evening.

"I'll call the station for a car when we are ready. Have you sent any men to inventory Gruber's shop?" asked John.

"Yes, they've been there all morning."

"Good. Then we'll talk later."

John wanted to go up to his room and collect his thoughts, but with so much to do he decided to walk back up to Gruber's pawnshop where he found three policemen going through a list of Gruber's inventory list and matching it with what they found on the shelves. Mullins and Tom Kitchen were upstairs quietly sprinkling fingerprint powder on apartment surfaces. Mrs. Llewelyn apparently had not returned.

John sat at Gruber's kitchen table and started making notes, yet he couldn't stop the face of Anne from crowding out everything.

Chapter 5

*"their cowed / Subjection to the ghosts of friends
who died,"*

(November 10, 1920—Afternoon)

About four o'clock the investigation had progressed as far as they could go. Nothing missing, according to Gruber's inventory, and Kitchen had finger-printed every surface in the apartment. With everyone at the fete and no one around to question, each had gone to freshen up before coming to the festival. They entered the old walled part of ancient York in a police car. Kitchen drove, dressed in his civilian clothes, a light grey three-piece suit, starched white shirt, maroon silk tie. His hair pomaded into submission and an attitude of assurance, which left no room for teasing, therefore, neither John nor Mullins mentioned his dapper look.

Fine crenelated, medieval walls had completely surrounded old York for maybe seven hundred years, but York's roots ran back two thousand years to when Romans stood here inside their garrison. A thousand years ago Vikings ruled the entire northern and eastern part of Britain from their capital at York.

John felt the enchantment of the Middle Ages as they passed from the twentieth century through a high, arched gate formed in the wall of huge, beige blocks of stone, twenty-five feet tall and ten feet thick. Two small round guard towers squatted at each corner of the gate where chain-mail-wearing guards had once peered through the long narrow, arrow slits, bravely protecting York from any outside evil.

Throngs of people heading to the festivities slowed their car to a crawl. They crept past small shops, some half-timbered, some red brick, and most with a second story that cantilevered out over the first floor, further closing in the narrow, cobbled road. Most of the shops they passed were closed or were about closing here as well as the shops on Holgate Street.

"We entered through Bootham Bar, the oldest gate, which goes back to Roman times," Kitchen informed them. "There's a walkway at the top of the wall which goes completely around Old Town. I think it's about three miles total. As grammar school students, we walked the whole of it once. Another gate round the other side is called 'Stonegate' because something near 20,000 tons of stone got drug up here from the riverside. All that stone to build the central tower of the minster."

Kitchen nodded his head in the direction of the minster. The square towers of York's Minster soared majestically on a hill off to their left dominating the entire walled city and dwarfing the small shops they drove past.

"This cathedral is actually called a 'minster.' Minster is an old word meaning they ministered to the people and taught them—or something like that."

Kitchen smiled sideways at John. "Sorry, sir. We learn all this in school 'round here, and we can't help telling newcomers all about it."

"Go on, Kitchen, it's interesting."

John thought about the 800-year-old familiar streets of his beloved Ayr. Only a few of the many ancient cities in Britain had such a finely preserved wall as York.

Kitchen pointed down a side street. "There's a tearoom right down that street that's been various kinds of businesses since the fourteenth century. Supposedly, one of the oldest buildings still being used anywhere in Europe."

The medieval atmosphere in Old Town York was enhanced by the number of people dressed in medieval costumes, including children with their parents and dozens of teens walking together. Several girls wore pastel, long shimmering dresses with pointed sleeves dropping nearly to their knees. Some wore tall pointed hats sheathed in gauzy material, billowing behind them in the breeze. The boys wore forest green tunics over tights bagging at the knees.

The three policemen wound their way around the tight curving streets, opening up to a large grassy square, filled today with colorful banners, booths, a puppet show, a clown, a man on stilts, some athletic competitions and a mass of people enjoying the pleasant November day.

"This is St. Sampson's Square," Kitchen continued. "It's kind of the hub of the area. It's always been the market."

John could picture people coming from miles around to sell their pigs and chickens and buy cloth, pots and pans, or other wares and to celebrate. He found it, indeed, hard not to fall under Old York's spell.

Kitchen parked the police car across from the square, to serve as a visual presence of the police, reminding any rowdies to beware. John and Mullins followed him to a booth where Chief Constable Weems stood, talking to a severe, no-nonsense looking woman. A smile transformed her whole face into a welcome once she spotted Kitchen, whom she obviously knew and had some affection for. The hand-painted sign over her booth proclaimed "Homemade Biscuits for Sale—Donations for St. Andrews Church."

Weems greeted them, shook hands, took the car keys from Kitchen, and introduced them to his wife, Mary.

"You boys look up to no good to me. And don't think you'll be getting any free biscuits merely since you're the law," she teased, forming her face back into a stern mask while handing each of them a sugary biscuit.

"Why don't you have a look round," Weems said munching on his strawberry biscuit. "I'll keep an eye out for anything notable that I see. If we lose track of each other, you know how to get back to your hotel?"

John nodded, already looking around.

"We'll get together first thing in the morning and compare notes," he said in a serious professional tone letting John know that his casual attitude didn't stop the policeman working.

John noted Weems seemed truly relaxed. The most uninvolved, unconcerned chief constable John had ever encountered. It didn't seem right, but he couldn't figure Weems out, why he's so disconnected to this case.

"Please find who killed Hans, Inspector Ferguson," Mary Weems said. "He was a good man and a friend who will be missed by a lot of people."

"Oh, I almost forgot to tell you about David." Weems said, "David Gruber, got back in town and told me Hans's will is going to be read tomorrow at one o'clock. I'll send Kitchen to find you—if there's any chance, that is, that he won't be stuck to you. He's pretty impressed with you."

Kitchen turned bright red, even his ears flamed with embarrassment. He didn't know whether to smile or not. It was impossible to tell from the chief's tone if he approved or disapproved of the young man's enthusiasm.

John's jaw clenched. He knew Kitchen would be disappointed if he failed—and Mullins's disillusionment would be crushing to him. It would have been easier to work with some jaded old cop. Someone he couldn't let down.

"I could use some more men working on this, especially since the rest of this day will probably not produce much." John said, frustrated.

"I'll see what I can do. We're not a large force, Ferguson."

John would learn what he could by mingling with the crowd. The idea was to observe the common citizens of York interacting with each other from a distance, without drawing ill feelings toward the police. The festive atmosphere could be to his advantage.

His gaze fell on Doctor and Mrs. Berry standing alone near a tea table, dolefully drinking their tea. The exuberant fun whirling around them seemed not to touch the couple at all.

John asked, "Weems, do you know why the Berrys seem so, well, hostile about our investigation of Gruber's death? Dr. Berry omitted from his autopsy report that Gruber had been knocked out by ether before his death."

"I know, Kitchen told me. The Berrys haven't been the same since Stanley died in France. A lot of people are different now."

Anne, standing across the square, captured John's gaze. His heart leaped.

John's focus returned to the Berrys when Mullins asked, "But would their sorrow cause them to commit murder only because Mr. Gruber was German?"

"I don't think so," Weems said.

John thought it sounded like Weems hoped more than believed it wasn't true.

"Well then, we'll see you tomorrow, Weems."

John excused them and told Mullins. "Mingle and listen. I am going to talk to Anne Winthrop some more."

Mullins nodded earnestly and walked off across the square, mumbling, "Mingle and listen, mingle and listen." He walked hesitantly, meandering, as he pondered how he should carry out his orders to mingle and listen. Then, making a decision, he marched straight toward a booth selling sausages and placed his order.

John watched Mullens and smiled. It reminded him of his own hunger. Mrs. Weems' free biscuit hadn't been enough to fill him up.

John spotted men in the crowd wearing their military uniforms, rifles swung over their shoulders, laughing and talking as friends and family admired them. The parade must have recently ended. He had watched soldiers march in parades since his return to reality, an endless number of parades. They marched bravely with mock fierceness down avenues and across squares. People cheered. Proud men who had been to war, concealing the unspeakable truths they had discovered that no one wanted to learn and finally deciding they had a right to expect people's admiration. Each parade disgusted John. The millions of cold and dead under Flanders fields were being mocked. Their ghosts exorcised from soldiers' dreams. What did their deaths mean when each returning soldier abandoned his ghoulish tales of war, and men refused to howl for their companions? Dead countrymen who, it seemed to John, had died for nothing. And yet, he knew he also lacked the courage to shout the truth in the faces of those who didn't want to hear it. But he at least kept it in his heart, where it whispered always in his dreams.

A parade soldier having trouble with his helmet chinstrap, which interfered with his pint of ale, handed his rifle to a boy of about fourteen while he took off his helmet and put it on the lad's head. The crowd smiled and clapped.

John shook his head and pushed past them. Tomorrow, a huge parade will commence in London, leading to the burial of one nameless, faceless dead man who will be honored to represent all the unknown soldiers. Possibly Dr. Berry's son, Stanley.

He walked away from the soldiers and stepped up silently beside Anne, observing her closely. Chestnut brown hair struck through with red high-lights, blowing slightly back in her face. Luscious red lips painted more

London fashion than what he observed in York. He followed her gaze to the shot-put contest.

"Good afternoon, Inspector. Giving it a rest for the day?" she said without turning to look at him. "Do you think if you stare at me long enough you'll be able to tell if I'm guilty of something?"

"Sorry." He dropped his eyes to his shoes and could feel his face redden, something a woman hadn't made him do for many years.

Anne turned and grinned up at him.

"I, or we rather, are observing people."

Brilliant. After a year dreaming about this woman, I am practically speechless in her presence.

Anne's interest in the shot-put returned and she clapped as a handsome man about thirty with black curly hair stepped up to throw, limping slightly. The applause became more enthusiastic for this strong, barrel-chested man with muscular arms who the crowd favored.

The man threw Anne a dazzling smile, claiming her favor like a jousting knight. He wound up with the heavy ball tucked under his chin and unwound hurling it with a roar. It sailed a good two feet farther than a yellow flag marking the best throw so far. The cheering stopped abruptly when the man collapsed, holding his leg writhing in pain.

Anne ran to him as did others, including John.

"Owen, are you alright?" she asked.

He grimaced and rocked back and forth, trying to hide the extent of his pain.

John realized that something serious had occurred or else this strong man would be able to conceal his pain.

"Does anyone have a car to take this man to hospital?" John asked.

"I do," said one of the on-lookers, a tall slender man with a thick mustache, much like John's, who had been measuring throws. He now ran for his car. Several other men carried Owen to the car, while the car's owner stood in front of it and pulled up on the crank until it roared to life, then raced around the car, throwing the crank onto the floor as Owen was gently lowered onto the seat.

Owen searched for Anne among those surrounding him and told her, "Don't bother about me. Have some fun, Anne, for once. We'll talk later."

Then the car roared off out of St. Sampson's Square.

The crowd thinned and John braved a glance at Anne as she stared after the car.

"He'll be alright, I'm sure," he said to her.

"Oh, I'm sure he will. But now I don't know what I should do. We were going to the dance together after the shot-put contest—my first dance for ever so long. I guess I should have gone with him. Now I should go home." Her face searched the crowd and stopped when she spotted Lisle.

John looked toward Lisle, who was standing next to the girl who had served their breakfast in the tearoom this morning. Will Parker, Tom Kitchen, DC Mullins, and two other young men tried to engage Lisle. John saw the girl from the tearoom—*What's her name, Alice that's it.* She animatedly tried to get the boys' attention, but they ignored her and gaped at the radiant Lisle. John noted that Lisle remained apart even surrounded by the others.

Poor Alice, she's no match for Lisle, John thought.

"Perhaps Lisle and I should go home."

"Lisle looks like she is with her friends and isn't ready to go home yet."

"Do you think she's enjoying herself? It doesn't really look like she's having that much fun."

"Of course she is.

"Really? That would be wonderful. Lisle is always so responsible and adult. Don't you think a sixteen-year-old should simply be silly sometimes?"

Anne had obviously been worried about her.

John said, "Lisle has grown up already. She has been through things those young people will never have to go through, if they're lucky. It's hard to be silly when you've seen what she has."

Anne looked up into his face. "You were in the war too, weren't you?"

"I vote you go on into the dance." He tried to sound lighthearted. "There'll be plenty of people you know who'll want to ask a beautiful woman to dance."

And possibly some man who won't say such inane things, he thought.

"Perhaps you'll ask me to dance," she smiled up at him.

His heart fluttered. It actually fluttered.

No wonder people thought of hearts and love together.

"Um, I should mingle and listen," he told her. "But perhaps I can come in later." He tried to make his voice sound professional.

He decided to leave before he lost his power of speech altogether and only stood there drooling.

Anne smiled brightly. "Well, later then perhaps."

He wondered if she was laughing at him or merely amused by him, as she walked toward the hall where a band began playing. She waved to another woman and the two of them walked in together.

John searched the square, his gaze stopping on Will Parker, buying two drinks at one of the stands while Mrs. Berry approached and tapped Will on the shoulder. As he turned around, his smile evaporated. Mrs. Berry appeared to be quite angry. Will argued with her. Mrs. Berry turned abruptly and skulked back to her husband. Still holding his two drinks, Will scanned the crowd. John wondered what that had been about, but as he watched, Will spotted Lisle who had apparently ditched her entourage of young men from a few moments before. She walked aimlessly from booth to booth. Will walked up to her and handed her one of his drinks, using the same cocky grin and attitude John had first seen in the pub this morning.

Lisle took the drink, but she never looked directly at Will, nor did she respond to his animated conversation.

Will figured out she was not buying his charm. He lifted his drink as if in a toast to her and then stalked off.

Lisle's gaze returned to the Punch and Judy puppets she had been watching, but it didn't look as if they amused her any more than Will had done.

John surveyed the crowd until he spotted Mullins standing next to Kitchen and Alice. He couldn't tell if Mullins actually was working on the case or simply chatting, but he decided, first, he would find himself a sausage roll and some tea, then sit and observe the crowd awhile before checking up on his two young policemen.

Twenty minutes later, Mullins sat down next to him. "I've been mingling and listening, sir. I talked to Will, Tom Kitchen, Lisle, and Alice. I don't think I've discovered anything important. Alice is the girl who works in the hotel tea shop and she's jealous of Lisle and says nasty things about her whenever she can. Will and Tom both are smitten with the fabulous Lisle."

"Fabulous, is she?"

"Well, she would be fabulous, except we all seem to bore her. She gives the impression that we are far beneath her glorious self. I rather enjoyed some of Alice's tart remarks."

"Like what?"

"Oh, I don't know. Like Lisle is too in love with herself to fall in love with any man."

"And you, of course, weren't trying to impress the fabulous Lisle."

Mullins's eyes found Lisle walking alone. "Well, perhaps a little." His voice faded with longing.

Lisle was breathtaking. Her straight blond hair shimmered in the sunlight. It fell halfway down her back, and people turned to look at her, simply to admire a beautiful young woman.

John wondered about Lisle. Earlier when he first met her, she seemed genuinely bubbly and happy around Anne and her son, Eddie. But all the silly fun that the others were having seemed to elude her here. He decided he would have a chat with her and instructed Mullins to find Kitchen and go into the hall where the music could be heard, softly, from where they stood.

"I want both you and Kitchen to be listening to what people are talking about."

John walked across the square towards Lisle as Mullins walked toward the hall. While she appeared oblivious to those around her, as he got closer, he observed her intense awareness of her surroundings. She wasn't bored. She was alert in the way that soldiers and police officers are trained to be. Attentive and wary. Danger could be anywhere.

"Hello, Lisle."

She tensed as soon as she recognized who he was.

"What do you want?"

"I'm wondering where little Eddie is this afternoon—and Anne's mother? Aren't they coming to the fete?"

She relaxed a bit. "Eddie and I were over here earlier. We had hardly arrived when you came to the pharmacy to interrogate us."

"Interrogate you? I only asked some questions. Don't you want me to find out who murdered Mr. Gruber?"

"Anne doesn't like you asking questions. It made her angry that you got *Mamie* upset."

"*Mamie?* Isn't that French for granny?"

"Yes, it is."

"Do you call Mrs. Thornton '*Mamie*'?"

"Yes. Anne worries about *Mamie's* health."

Lisle started walking. John kept stride. They walked alone on the grass and stopped at the back of a crowd watching a juggler.

"Anne didn't seem to like Mr. Gruber much. Do you know why?"

"He was not nice to *Mamie*."

"Really? What did he do to her?"

"I don't know. Why don't you ask Anne?"

"I will. Lisle, did you have any reason to hate Mr. Gruber? Did he ever bother you in any way?"

Her stare reflected the burned-out hollowness, John guessed, from her experiences with soldiers in Belgium. Ten years old when the war left her an orphan and homeless. He knew how she had kept from starving. He pictured the hundreds of hungry pleading eyes he had seen at the sides of the roads, their hands out, begging for anything from the soldiers as they rode or walked past from one battle to the next. A beautiful little girl growing into a beautiful young woman at the mercy of men made brutish by their own struggle to survive. Germans going one direction, British, French, and Americans going the other direction down the roads of Lisle's Belgium.

She knew exactly why he asked her about Mr. Gruber bothering her.

"No," she said simply and emphatically. She needed to say nothing more. He believed that Gruber had never touched her.

"And where is *Mamie*?"

"She and Eddie are both staying with Mrs. Llewelyn next door, at the butcher's. That way Anne and I can enjoy our evening."

"Are you enjoying yourself, Lisle? Are you going to the dance?"

"Yes," she said, raising a small smile.

John could sympathize with someone trying to forget the war and relearn about this thing called "fun."

"Could I walk you over?"

"Thank you, no. I'm not altogether finished looking at everything out here."

Right. Besides I could be acting inappropriately towards her as far as she is concerned. Flirting with her to gather information would not be productive.

John would tell Mullins and Kitchen the same thing as soon as he found them. Looking around, he saw no familiar faces and decided it was time to observe the people inside at the dance.

Directly in front of him, across the dance floor, Anne argued with Will Parker. She flashed a mixture of revulsion and rage. The loud dance music drowned out their conversation. She slapped his face, which surprised him so much that his beer slipped from his hand and crashed to the floor. The sudden noise caused the people near to turn towards the noise. She raised her hands to her face covering her embarrassment. Will snarled something to her before storming off, leaving Anne glaring after him with a look of disbelief. Friends came over out of curiosity and to help her clean up the mess. She smiled nervously as she chatted with them.

Another person Will Parker seems to have made angry. I'll question her as soon as the group around her leaves.

Near the far end of the room, away from the band, Dr. and Mrs. Berry talked to Chief Constable Weems and his wife in a smiling and friendly manner, not even noticing Anne's drama. The chief glanced up and nodded at John.

John couldn't figure Weems out. He had hardly become the chief constable of a city the size of York by standing around waiting for someone to direct him and hoping others would solve crimes for him. Then John spotted DC Mullins.

Mullins lurked, conspicuously, behind the refreshment table, much too close, to eavesdrop on two men talking. They glanced over their shoulders a couple of times then moved off a few seconds later shaking their heads. Before John could reach him through the crowd, Mullins had moved in on five women in their sixties, talking and laughing behind their hands as they watched the dancers. He leaned in to hear their conversation. When one woman noticed him, they turned on him, shouting and shooing him away.

"What exactly do you think you're doing, DC Mullins?"

"I'm mingling and listening, sir."

Hearing Mullins say it made his instructions sound as silly as when he had said them to Anne.

"Discreetly overhear from a respectable distance, Mullins!"

That hadn't sounded any better.

"Look, Mullins. You're sticking your nose practically in their faces and ruffling their feathers! No one is going to be saying anything of importance about our case while you're skulking around. Try to act naturally."

"I can't hear what they're saying with the band playing and all, unless I get that close."

"Perhaps it's time to take a break, at least, until the band takes a break. And where is Kitchen?"

"Dunno, sir." He craned his head around. "He's here someplace."

"And no more listening and mingling. Simply observe, all right?"

Mullins focused on John's instructions. "Right then," he said, turning and marching into the crowd, looking left and right in a ridiculous and obvious manner.

Shaking his head, John turned away from Mullins to find Kitchen and see how he fared when he noticed Will Parker standing alone near him, staring intently somewhere over John›s shoulder. He turned to discover Lisle rushing to help Anne.

"She's a beautiful young woman, isn't she?" John said quietly as he stepped up behind him.

Without taking his eyes off Lisle, Will nodded.

"Are you and Lisle going out together?" John tried not to sound prying.

"We're about to be." Will tore his gaze from her and blinked a couple of times. "I hope," he added with a weak smile.

John saw Lisle put her arm on Anne's shoulder. Anne smiled, shaking her head, appearing to try to convince the girl that she was fine.

Anne took Lisle by the shoulders, turned her around, practically in Tom Kitchen's face.

The stocky young man with the dark mane of hair started backing up, apologetically, until Lisle smiled at him and said something. His face beamed. Taking her arm he steered her to the dance floor as the band played yet another waltz, encouraging couples to dance.

Anne's face beamed as she watched them dance.

Will turned from them, jealous of Kitchen's success, and walked out a side door with John following him. Will lit a cigarette and inhaled deeply.

"What were you and Anne arguing about a minute ago?"

"Really, that's none of your business, Inspector."

"It is if it has to do with what you know about Hans Gruber's murder."

Now he had Will's complete attention. "It had nothing to do with anything you need to be concerned about."

John could ask Anne later when he spoke to her. "Does Anne disapprove of you asking Lisle out?"

"No. Why would she? That's ridiculous."

"Perhaps Hans Gruber disapproved of you and Lisle and threatened you if you attempted to see her?"

"You have a vivid imagination, Inspector. Why would anyone not want me to see Lisle?"

"Will, describe for me in detail what you saw when you pushed open Gruber's back door. Everything you saw and heard." John watched Will's reaction to this sudden change in subject.

Will's countenance shifted as he visualized the scene. "I...I stepped into the dark. Total quiet, eerie like. I don't know what made me go to the stairs instead of turning around or calling out to old Gruber or what."

Perhaps you came to steal something, John thought, but didn't want to interrupt.

"I crept up the stairs. My eyes adjusted to the dark, and I could barely make out the top of the steps. Don't ask me how, but I knew something was wrong. No way Gruber just happened to leave his back door open. At the top of the stairs, light from the street coming through his office window lit that room enough for me to see a little. I couldn't see a thing in the rest of the pitch-black apartment, so I stepped through the doorway of his office, found the switch and turned on the light. All that blood." He shook his head in a manner John thought was genuine, upset at the memory. "All that blood." He looked directly into John's eyes. "Behind me from somewhere in the dark, I heard someone bolt down the stairs."

John thought of the lurking housekeeper. "Could it have been the woman who worked for him?"

"Mrs. Llewelyn? Maybe but that doesn't seem right. And besides, she's always gone home before then."

Why would Will Parker know her schedule, John wondered, *unless maybe he had been planning a robbery—or a murder?*

"The person seemed quicker somehow than her. Anyway, I was scared, believe you me. I froze for a second, maybe there are more of them, and here I am a witness—or maybe he only stopped at the bottom of the stairs and was waiting for me to come back down. Before I scared myself useless, I bolted faster than a hare. I didn't even realize my screaming and blubbering alerted everyone in the pub. Believe me I didn't want to do that. And then some of them drunken sods ran over there. Something none of them would have done sober, I can tell you."

John believed Will had been terrified by the blood and the body, not to mention whoever he had surprised. The murderer.

"Will, you may have seen the murderer. Can you tell me anymore about the person? Did it seem to be a man, do you think?"

Will thought. "Truly, I can't, Inspector. I didn't see anything. I only heard him run. I guess it could even have been Mrs. Llewelyn if she was scared enough. Believe me I would tell you if I knew. Nobody deserves to die like that."

John felt convinced Will wasn't the murderer, yet felt he could still tell him more. Perhaps he knew someone who wanted Gruber dead.

"You hear a lot of angry men in the pub. Anyone you can think of?"

Will turned and did not answer.

John knew whatever he was withholding wouldn't be in his best interest to share with a policeman. He would question him tomorrow at the police station alone and maybe get better results.

"Thank you," John said, which Will took for a dismissal and walked down the steps away from the building and across the square.

John turned to reenter the dance. Anne appeared at the doorway, smiling when she saw him.

"Oh, Inspector, I didn't know you were out here. I thought I might step outside for a moment. It's getting stuffy inside."

Her smile warmed him. Straight white teeth. John watched as she wet her full, red-painted lips with her tongue. Greenish-grey eyes gazed up from beneath long dark lashes, exploring his face and down his body. Her blue dress shimmered, shorter than most other young women's, reached barely to her knees. Her silk stockings showed her slim legs unlike the modest black stockings he had seen most often worn here today.

"Are you glad you stayed for the dance?" he asked.

"I don't know yet. I'll have to let you know. Actually I might leave."

"Did whatever Will say to you spoil your evening?"

"No, not really."

"What upset you so?"

"Nothing really. It's just that he is so vulgar, and it upsets me when he asks about Lisle. I really don't want her around the likes of Will Parker. I want her to be happy."

When John looked back through the doorway, Kitchen and Lisle were standing at the refreshment table, listening to an apparently riveting story told by Mullins, who had temporarily forgotten his stealthy posturing.

John brought his attention back to the conversation with Anne, "She seems to be genuinely enjoying herself now."

Anne came over and stood directly in front of him, her back brushing against him, to see where he was looking. Her perfume had a dusky, knowing quality to it.

"Yes, I think she is doing quite well," she said.

"We could ask Kitchen and Mullins to watch out for her while I walk you home and perhaps ask you a few questions. She couldn't be safer than with two policemen watching out for her."

Anne turned around, the top of her head grazing his lips. She looked up into his face and put her hand on his arm. "That sounds like a good idea," she said.

Mullins and Kitchen were delighted by the idea of walking Lisle home later. Lisle smiled and said she thought it a wonderful idea. Kitchen and Mullins promised to have her home as soon as the dance ended. Anne relaxed. She retrieved her jacket and led John out the side door. The brisk air hit them and they buttoned up. Winter grew close. He noted they left by the opposite side of the square from where he had arrived.

She led him out of Old York in a new direction that he would remember, just as he would remember how Kitchen had led them to the square earlier.

Dark rain clouds raced to overshadow the emerging stars, and the day's last rim of orange illuminated the faces of those dismantling the stalls that lined the festival grounds. Faces and voices, mellow and contented from a day that had fulfilled their expectations.

"Tell me about your mother and Mr. Gruber," John asked as they walked.

She sighed, then started to speak, slowly at first, unwilling to talk about something unpleasant.

"The Grubers and my parents had known each other since before I was born. Hans' wife died years ago but he remained friends with my mother and father. Then he died. My wonderful father died." Her voice became softer as she spoke of her father. "He always encouraged me to try things as a girl and always praised me when I did. When I married, he paid for Peter to become a licensed pharmacist to ensure our future. We were so happy, and then it completely started to fall apart. Peter worked in our pharmacy with Father until one day Father suddenly died of a heart attack."

The wind picked up whipping through the narrow streets stinging their faces. Around them people hunched in their coats and hurried along the street. Anne appeared not to notice.

"Then Peter stupidly decided he must fight in that awful war—for his country. He'd never forgive himself if he didn't join the army. He left Mother and me alone to fight for what? To die for what?" She almost spat out the words. "He almost made it home unharmed, and then within a couple of months of the end he suffered horrible burns during some battle. They sent him to hospital in Nottingham and I stayed with him but it was so horrible. When they changed his bandages, he looked like meat, like burned black meat. His fingers and ears had burned off. He screamed with pain every day."

Anne stopped talking and they turned down another unfamiliar street, each turn narrower than the last. Far behind, the minster loomed black above the rooftops. The darkness hid her face from John's view.

"I hoped he would die. Isn't that terrible? And not solely because of all his pain, but I couldn't bear the repulsive thought of him ever touching me again. Then he did die after fighting so hard for months to live. I felt so guilty and relieved at the same time. And I brought his body home to be buried."

John pictured her standing at the station with her hand on his coffin.

"I hate war. Why did the Germans do that to us?" Her voice was filled with hatred.

"And Hans Gruber was a German."

"What? No. He had always lived here—for my whole life. I can't imagine—well, no one blamed him for the war. Do you believe someone murdered him because he was German?"

"I don't know. Without your father and husband, you and your mother had to figure out how to survive. What did you do?"

Anne turned left down a barely visible passageway between two buildings, then left again down a dark, foreboding alley, so narrow and dark that John thought they could be walking into another dimension. The only sound came from their feet crunching the gravel as they continued along the deepening darkness, then a door opened to their right, startling John into stopping. A golden glow from inside lit a medieval knight in armor holding a sword. He glared at John for a second, made a disgusted grunting sound, and slammed the door, returning them to darkness.

Anne, absorbed in her thoughts, hadn't slowed her pace, leaving John standing alone to wonder if the man had been real. Perhaps he had just seen a ghost that had been left behind five hundred years ago, to protect York for all eternity.

John and Anne stepped into a well-lit street that appeared out of the darkness, with people scurrying home before the storm hit. He looked behind them to see that they had emerged between two shops from a space so slight and hidden, it appeared they merely popped back from medieval times into the present. Anne obviously knew these tortuously intertwined back alleys quite well. He wasn't sure he could find this way again, but they were now on the same street that Kitchen drove this morning, and John found himself happy to be oriented again. They emerged near the wall and he could see Bootham Bar, the city gate they had entered earlier.

He led Anne towards the gate.

Anne stopped in her tracks. "Mr. Gruber forced Mother to become his lover in exchange for his help. They thought I didn't know, but I could hear her leave, creep down the stairs in the dark, late at night. I watched out my window as he let her into his shop. He knew that without a licensed pharmacist, we became only an herb shop. You know, home remedies. We've always sold a lot of herbs. They're a lot cheaper than prescription drugs, and now with money tight we sell more than ever. But we couldn't live on the income from herbal remedies alone. Gruber offered to pay for me to become licensed. We had to borrow from him to stay in business, and I jumped at the idea of a way out of debt. At first, I didn't realize the price for our shop resulted in my mother becoming his mistress. He pretended to help an old friend, so I studied in London and got my degree while Mother took care of Eddie. I eventually figured out his plot as I watched her night after night during breaks from school." Anne spoke with bitterness.

"When I finally got on the train to come home with my degree in hand, I raced back, glad to tell mother she would no longer be enslaved by him. I would take care of us, but she had her stroke the day I got home."

"And then Gruber's concern and help stopped?"

"No. He waited like a vulture for his prey to get well so he could continue where he left off," she said with disgust.

"Well, actually a vulture waits, hoping his prey will die—not get well."

"What?"

"Nothing." They walked through the tall arched town gate and along the outside of the formidable wall for a block before crossing the street to the alley behind the chemist shop, leaving mysterious medieval York behind.

Only lit from the corner streetlight, the alleyway became darker as they approached her door, and he couldn't tell which door belonged to her. All similar, the doors had no identifying markings.

Anne stopped and unlocked a substantial door, strong as all the doors were to protect the shops from burglary. She held the door, inviting him in. He shut out the cold behind them.

"Would you like some tea?"

"Yes, that would be nice." They took off their coats.

John sat at the small table, wondering if he should admit to her that they had met before. He watched while she lit a match on the stove under the kettle. They both waited, immersed in their own thoughts while the water heated and the tea steeped in the tiny kitchen. He knew he couldn't stop himself much longer from talking about it, and this moment was more relaxed and private than tomorrow would be with Mullins and Kitchen around. She filled two cups with tea and sat down stirring some sugar into hers.

"Sugar, John?"

"Thanks."

He stirred the sugar into his tea and took a deep breath. "Anne, I knew about your husband being dead. When you brought him home that evening on the train, you and I had a conversation. Do you recall our discussion?"

She looked puzzled.

"I was the soldier in the compartment on the train with you. Anne, you have been in my thoughts often since that extraordinary night."

"Stars eavesdropping on our silly lives," she said evenly.

"Yes. Well, that's what we said anyway. You remember?"

"And you said life is good. You just back from war, and me burying my husband, and a crazy stranger says 'life is good.' Yes, I remember."

"It lingers as one of the loveliest, most powerful experiences of my life. Maybe it was because I had just been released from hospital that our meeting meant so much to me. I wanted to find you and make sure you were alright. I got stronger to…to I don't know what. I wanted to see you again and show you that living your life is better than giving up."

"We can't change anything from the past or know the future. We have only tonight. Do you remember me saying that?"

He nodded.

"And I kissed you. You kissed me back."

He nodded. "I wanted to take away all the ugliness in your life."

"Then make the ugliness go away now, John."

He stood up and reached for her. She took his hand without a word and led him upstairs to her bedroom.

A small voice in the back of his head warned him that Scotland Yard inspectors don't do this sort of thing. Ever. But she stood so close to him. He held her against him and kissed her. A kiss she returned with an equal passion to his own.

Anne sighed and a tiny moan escaped her lips. The same moan that had haunted him since the night on the train, only this time it belonged to him. She would be making love to him, not a shadow, not a memory. His small voice quieted.

An hour later John walked in full darkness through a light, cold rain, back down the alley and across to the Green Man Hotel, thinking of their touching and soft murmuring, still smelling her.

The night clerk handed John his room key, a message to call Howell. He glanced across the lobby at the tearoom and watched a man putting the chairs up on the tables. If he wanted something to eat, he would have to go to the pub, but he wasn't hungry enough to walk to the other end of the block. Howell would probably have gone home by now, he rationalized, and they had made precious little headway in the case. He decided to put off the call to Howell until morning.

John walked up to his room, worked on his notes or at least wrote the facts from today's investigation. He found that he couldn't concentrate on the murder that brought him to York. Seeing the connections between random facts eluded him and he couldn't find any discrepancies in statements. He kept thinking about the beautiful, passionate Anne. He gave up and fell, exhausted, into bed, feeling healed and strong, happy even. He slept and dreamt the recurrent dream of the restaurant with the green and white striped awning

He stood on the street looking in the window. The awning flapped loudly, snapping and moaning a warning as the wind tore at it, all else around him became silent. A couple ate quite contentedly. The sinister, clown-faced maître d' appeared suddenly in his face.

"You can't come in here yet, Captain. You're not dead, not yet."

The clown laughed maniacally and looked up behind John.

Following his gaze, John watched in horror as soldiers dropped out of the sky, ripping apart the awning, smashing their bodies onto the sidewalk in front of the café. Screaming, dying. Young soldiers piling up on top of each other, blood everywhere. Two of the men falling were Tom Kitchen and Patrick Mullins. He could hear their pleas for help. They cried, "Please don't let us die. You can save us. We know you can! We trust you!"

John awoke, his heart pounding with the young men's pleas ringing in his head. A weak morning light shimmered through the lace curtains at his window. Someone pounded on his door.

"Hold on, I'm coming." When he opened the door, Mullins and Tom Kitchen stood there.

"Sir, you need to come. They've found Will Parker's body at the bottom of the wall of the old city. It looks like someone threw him off."

Looking at their faces, John thought, *God, I can't save anyone—not even myself.*

Chapter 6

"Their dreams that drip with murder";

(November 11, 1920—7:00 am)

Constable Kitchen again drove the three men inside the Old Town wall, only this time he turned left. The Minster sat high on its misty hill. Its austere spires, vague outlines hidden by a lingering mist not yet vanquished by the morning sun. It felt like the beginning of another crisp, clear day. John recognized the name "Goodramgate Street" as they passed. He and Anne had walked down it the night before. This morning, however, they stopped at the foot of a section of the wall and walked over to Weems, who stood next to Will Parker's body where it lay crumpled at the bottom of the walkway. The walkway, Kitchen told them yesterday, encircled the top of the entire wall.

The scene conjured no medieval images this morning. The violent present became gruesomely real.

"Morning, Ferguson," Weems said. "Looks like poor young Will fell or was pushed off the walkway right up there."

The wooden railing appeared to be substantial. Scarcely a place for a person to stumble and fall over the edge. However, with enough alcohol, anything turned out to be possible. Weems walked John, Mullins, and Kitchen over to a rock retaining wall, four feet high and fifteen feet long, that held the sloping grassy area next to the wall from eroding away. The retaining wall ran parallel to the city wall above it and had a jagged top edge where a splash of blood smeared and dripped down the face of the rock ending at Will's body. This stood as the only place in either direction where the retaining wall jutted out dangerously under the walkway. Everywhere else the retaining wall continued underneath the walkway abutting glistening green grass, still wet from last night's rain. If Will had landed anywhere else, the soft grass would have broken his fall.

John asked both Mullins and Kitchen, "When did you two last see Will last night?"

They looked at one another, then Mullins spoke.

"He sort of circled us for a while, scowling at us. We both stayed pretty close to Lisle. He never came over to speak to her or us. She didn't seem to notice, and we certainly didn't care."

Kitchen added, "He prowled around the crowd irritating certain people, I noticed. Then he disappeared."

"Irritated them? How?"

Kitchen answered, "Oh, he seemed to find certain people, say something to them and they would get angry. Then he had that smile of his and he would move off. It didn't seem random though. He knew who he wanted to talk to."

Weems asked, "Did you know any of the people he talked to?"

"Some, yeah," Kitchen said. "That tailor fellow, Wilson. Then he talked to Mrs. Benson until Mr. Benson came over. You know how big he is. All he had to do was make a fist and ole Will made himself scarce."

John asked, "Does anyone know what Will planned or thought? I saw him anger both Dr. Berry and Anne Winthrop. She claims nothing important took place. Obviously, it is important."

Weems shrugged and shook his head, ending the discussion as far as it concerned him. He ordered Kitchen over to aid two constables already combing the grassy area surrounding the retaining wall. Up on the wall two more searched the walkway for clues. The railing didn't appear damaged.

John asked, "Who found the body, Weems?"

"A groundskeeper, Mr. Collins, over there." He pointed to a short, slight, older man with longish grey hair standing near the edge of the crime scene holding his hat in his hands, "I asked him to wait until you got here, that you might want a couple of words with him."

"DC Mullins, would you please take a statement from Mr. Collins and then let him go about his business?" John asked.

Mullins looked surprised but pleased with his assignment and took his notebook from his pocket as he walked toward Mr. Collins.

Last night's dream of the soldier, Mullins, begging him for help before he smashed into the pavement flashed across John's consciousness. Disgusted, he turned away from it. Yet, he couldn't shake the sadness he felt since he awoke.

"I need to inspect Will's body before it's taken away."

They stepped back to the body and turned it face up. A long, deep gash lay open along his right temple and blood dripped across his face. More blood pooled on the ground. So many sightless dead eyes of young men exactly like Will Parker's formed only memories for John, no flashback.

Anne's doing, he thought.

Will's body smelled of liquor. He had been drinking a lot yesterday.

John asked Weems, "Do you have any idea why he would be walking around up there late at night?"

A shake of the head said he didn't.

"Are you taking him to Dr. Berry for the autopsy?"

Weems nodded looking toward the nearby ambulance. "We're ready to send him to St. Mary's unless you need to see anything else first."

"Have his pockets been checked?"

"Yes. Nothing especially interesting." Weems produced a small bag which John emptied into his hand. A wallet, two one-pound coins, three shillings, and a key. John took the key and put it in his vest pocket. The wallet held only Will's identification and a small recent photo of Lisle playing with Eddie.

Weems took the photograph from John's hand. "See the stone wall behind Lisle? It looks like an old churchyard? I couldn't tell you which one though. All churchyards look alike then, don't they?"

John took the photo back nodding. "The minster?"

"I don't think so. It looks like a smaller and less cared for place. But maybe."

"I'm holding on to the key and this photo for now." John stood, slipping the photo in his pocket along with the key. "I guess I'll have to go tell Joseph Parker about his son now.

"Weems, we need to talk to the people at the festival who Will irritated last night," John said. "Someone has to tell us what's going on. Would you have Kitchen start interviewing them?"

John trusted Kitchen. He did not trust where Weems' loyalties lay.

"Of course, at once."

Weems motioned to the two men dressed in white, leaning against the ambulance looking bored. They brought a stretcher and wrapped the body in a sheet.

As they lifted Will, one of his lifeless hands flopped from under the sheet. Relaxed, slightly curled fingers that would never feel anything again. A white-hot jolt of terror exploded in John's brain then disappeared abruptly, leaving his heart racing, sweat pouring off his face.

Something about seeing that hand, but what?

John caught himself from going into a full-fledged flashback. Close to vomiting, if not screaming, he stumbled back. Realizing his hand covered his mouth, he dropped it to his side and looked around, wondering if anyone had noticed.

Only Weems stood nearby, and he was watching the ambulance men load the body.

Shaken by the sudden intense emotion of the near-flashback, John walked back to the police car. He needed to at least get a handle on what triggered the episode, then maybe he could avoid making a fool of himself. Bloody bodies, like the man in the Thames River and Gruber, didn't affect him, yet Will's hand unnerved him.

Weak and shaking, John scrambled into the backseat and told the constable to pick up Mullins, who was still talking to the caretaker, before taking them both to the Swan.

Mullins ducked into the back seat and sat next to John. "Mr. Collins is a groundsman and…what's wrong with you? You look like you've seen a ghost?"

There was no response whatever from John.

It happened again. Although Mullins had not witnessed it, he recognized the signs. Sallowness, perspiration. *Now I'm starting to worry. Maybe this is too much for him. What if his trying to focus on these bloody murders destroys what mental health he has? Maybe who I thought he was…maybe that's all gone now. Would it be ratting him out to tell Howell we need help?*

"What were you saying?" John came back to his senses.

"Mr. Collins, the groundsman, was checking the wall this morning around seven for debris left by drunken sods last night and he spotted Will's body. He ran to a nearby tea shop that he knew opened early and that had a telephone and called the police."

He couldn't help asking again, "You alright, sir?"

John nodded. "He starts work terribly early, doesn't he?"

"Apparently, sir."

Much improved by the time the constable left them in the alley behind The Swan, John stood behind Mullins as he pounded on the back door.

"All right, all right." Joseph Parker cracked the door and squinted at them. "Oh not you, Ferguson! What do you want now? I suppose your ridiculous questions and accusations against my boy can't wait until a decent hour of the morning?" Parker's hair stuck up in the back and he had stuffed his shirt into his trousers on one side. One suspender had been hurriedly snapped onto his shoulder.

"Mr. Parker, may we come in," John said gravely. "It's about Will."

Parker stopped short and, looking directly into John's eyes, opened the door.

John and Mullins sat in the pub's kitchen at the large work table, clean this morning, ready for another day. Parker stood clutching the back of a chair opposite them. His eyes pleaded.

John gently spoke. "I'm sorry to have to tell you, Mr. Parker, but we found Will dead this morning."

Parker braced himself. Yet the words struck him like a physical blow. His face crumpled, and he shook his head backing away from the shattering news.

John knew Parker wanted time to stop. Not to stop now but back to yesterday. Any time when life's cruelties and injustices and stupidities were bearable.

The pub and Parker evaporated from John's mind. For the first time, John remembered something real about the trauma at the Sommes that had landed him in hospital.

He remembered.

He stood in the mud on the battlefield in France. Someone was screaming. It was him. "No!" He screamed over and over before the curtain dropped on his sanity.

John drew himself back into the reality of the pub and Parker's devastated face as he realized Will was dead.

Mullins tried not to stare at the white knuckles of John's shaking, clasped hands.

Mullins could see no way of dismissing his senior officer's behavior.

John caught the fear and confusion in Mullins's face. He felt ashamed of himself for letting Will's lifeless hand pull him into the battlefield. He felt like an imposter, exposed in a disgusting lie, pretending to be something he hadn't been for some time, that is, a real detective inspector for Scotland Yard.

"What happened to Will, Ferguson?" Parker had composed himself and wanted to know the truth now.

"We're not sure at this point, Mr. Parker. He lay at the bottom of the Old Town wall where he apparently fell off the walkway. He fell against some jagged stones…I'm very sorry."

Parker stood, shoulders sagging, looking old and beaten. "That wall's not easy to fall off of, it seems to me." His shoulders straightened as he began to understand what John was saying. He didn't believe his son's death was accidental. "Someone's pushed him!"

"Can you think of anyone who might have wanted to push him over the edge of the walkway, or any reason why someone might do such a thing to him?"

Parker searched the faces of the men around him in the pub.

"Will was a…was a…spirited boy, Inspector, but he never got in any real trouble. He didn't hang around with a bad lot."

"Do you think he broke into Gruber's pawnshop or knew more than he told us about the murder?"

Parker dropped his defenses, focusing now on the death of his son. John could use his sudden candidness.

"I can't swear my son wasn't a thief, Inspector, maybe even planning something illegal, but I saw his face when he came roaring in here after seeing

Gruber's body, and believe me, it terrified him. Is this related to Gruber's murder? Did he see something he shouldn't have?"

John thought it quite possible.

"Could we see Will's room? See if we can find something that might help us figure out if he was indeed murdered, and if it's related to Mr. Gruber's death?"

Parker weighed his concern about policemen possibly finding something incriminating versus finding a clue which might lead to the murderer of his son.

Mullins nudged John's elbow.

John's gaze was drawn to the thirteen-year-old boy who had opened the door as they entered the pub the day before. The boy peered through a crack in the swinging door into the front of the pub, terrified, but unable to stop eavesdropping. Even through the cracks, the officers could see that he looked as though he wanted to cry, but his face had frozen into the first shocked reaction of hearing about Will.

Parker spotted the boy. "Charlie, what are you doing there?"

The boy stared. Then bolted upstairs.

"Charlie!"

"Who is Charlie?" John asked.

"He's my son. My younger son, Charlie. He worshiped his older brother. Wanted to be exactly like him."

Parker pursued Charlie up the stairs with John and Mullins trailing behind. Charlie disappeared into a room and slammed the door. Parker stopped.

"Will's room is up in the attic."

With John and Mullins at his heels, Parker continued in Charlie's direction, then turned, fished a key from his pants pocket, and handed it to John before continuing down the hall to talk with Charlie.

John and Mullins followed the narrow twist of stairs to the attic. John first tried the key the officers found in Will's pocket as he lay lifeless at the base of the tower. It did not open the door. Then he tried the key that Parker had just given him. It worked and opened the heavy arched door leading to the attic.

John pushed the heavy arched door open with the iron ring set in the center, revealing a small dormer room. The ceiling, barely tall enough in the center to stand in, slanted to walls only four feet high at the sides. One tiny window allowed a spot of morning light to brighten the room. Against one wall sat a narrow single bed neatly made with a threadbare blanket carefully tucked in. A seaman's humpbacked chest, clad in iron bands clasped shut with a large black lock squatted under the window. The key in John's pocket did not open it. A small bureau with three drawers stood against the opposite wall. On top of the bureau lay a hairbrush and a cup with shaving gear and a toothbrush.

John searched the bureau and found only clothes folded neatly, while Mullins searched under the bed, uncovering an extra pair of shoes, some boots, and a cardboard box covered in white satin. He dumped the contents of the box onto the bed, while John searched the pockets of two coats on a hook on the back of the door. Mullins opened the satin box and found a box camera and numerous pictures, including buildings, corners of buildings near sidewalk level, street scenes of people caught walking up streets as cars drove down them, a picture of a single lamppost, and the same lamppost evaporating through the fog at night.

"Strange pictures," Mullins said. Then he speculated, "Maybe these are pictures of places to rob or people to rob."

John picked up several of the photos. One picture depicted the corner of a building where a courageous flower grew from within a crack where the building met the sidewalk. The next photo revealed the back of a young woman holding the hand of a little girl. Both disappearing into the fringe of dark fog and out of the safe circle of light cast by the lamppost.

"The photos are…what? Artful, maybe." John said.

He wondered if he imagined the artistic quality.

A poetic punk?

John doubted the photos lead to crimes though.

Mr. Parker moved into the doorway. John handed him the photographs. Parker's puzzled expression showed that he had never seen the photos before and couldn't explain them.

Mullins asked, "Do you have a key to the trunk there?"

Parker stared at the trunk as if he had never seen it and shook his head.

"Ferguson, that knife Will found in the alley. Maybe it belongs to Llewelyns. You know. The butcher shop."

"Owen Llewelyn." John nodded. He hadn't met the strong man Anne had expected to accompany her to the dance yesterday until he was rushed away with an injured leg during shot put. It was the injury that had allowed John to be with Anne at the festival—and after.

Parker nodded at the name. "That's an expensive knife. Like a butcher would have."

"Where is Will? Where have they taken him? I have to tell his mother where he is."

"He'll be at the morgue across the street at St. Mary's. They'll call you soon. Right now, Mr. Parker, I need that trunk open,"

"Do you think he was murdered, Ferguson?" He asked for the second time.

John thought it was murder, but avoided the question.

"Can you tell me why he angered so many people he approached yesterday? What did he say? It might be a motive for murder."

"I didn't know he annoyed anyone. Some money-making scheme, I'd bet. But I have no idea about his plan."

"Helping us get into his locked chest might help us find out what his scheme involved. Who were his mates? Who went along with his schemes?"

"No one I knew about. He liked working alone on his ventures." Parker added, "Find the bastard, Ferguson. My son didn't deserve to be thrown off no wall and he didn't just happen to fall, neither."

"I will," John promised. "Right now, I will see the butcher and ask him about his knife." He left Mullins to open and check the trunk.

John walked to the police station, noted Weems was not back from Old Town, signed out the murder weapon, and went to find the butcher. From half a block away, between Dr. Berry's surgery on the corner and Anne's chemist shop, he watched Owen Llewelyn open the butcher shop door and set a sign out on the sidewalk. The strong man's right leg in a cast since reinjuring his war wound during the shot-put event at the festival, he hopped back into the shop awkwardly.

John stepped through the butcher shop's front door as the gleam of an enormous cleaver flashed, crashing down, shattering bone with a dull whack, the blade ending its arc by slicing through a red, raw slab of meat. Owen Llewelyn loosened the blade and teased the cut from the carcass, pushing it aside leaving a smear of blood on the scarred table. He looked up with a shopkeeper's smile before he saw who had entered.

"You are the man from Scotland Yard investigating old Gruber's death, right?"

John nodded.

"Also, the man who helped me get a ride to hospital yesterday. Did you enjoy the festivities?"

"Well, work took us there. Trying to learn something about the people who knew Gruber by observing them together."

"Did you learn something useful about us?" Llewelyn had an open and friendly manner, interested, not sarcastic or defensive.

"Probably. But right now I'm not sure what. How is your leg?"

Owen's face clouded with frustration, "Oh, doc's encased me in plaster again. It'll never be right, like before the war, and I always think I can do what I did then. This bum leg is compliments of a little battle known as the 'Somme.'"

"Amazing! I fought at the Somme. The second battle?"

The butcher nodded.

John had, up to now, discovered no one else who had fought in the same battle.

Llewelyn became somber. "You still dream about that bloody noise?"

Stunned, John simply nodded.

"Sometimes I wake up unable to breathe," Llewelyn reflected. "Afraid they'll never order the retreat, and I'll be buried alive in that goddamned trench with the rats."

John's mind fogged with the memory of scrambling out of his trench into the still dark morning.

He caught his breath and returned to reality. "The confusion with the ceaseless noise of the German cannon. I yelled at my men, but no one could hear me." John's memory ended with darkness and chaos. He tugged himself back into the conversation with Owen Llewelyn. "The retreat. Tell me about the retreat." He yearned to learn about the retreat, and yet knowing frightened him.

Llewelyn looked skeptical. "You don't remember that part?"

"I was…wounded then and I don't remember."

"Maybe forgetting is better. What I remember is being so terrified, men yelling orders, trying to save equipment and running before dawn from the German advance. It got light and we marched until we were ready to drop, always looking over our shoulder. Expecting death to catch us. German death. Sometime in there a huge piece of shrapnel nearly took my leg off, and I lost consciousness. My last thought—Thank God, I'm finally dead and out of it. I won't be terrified or tired or thirsty anymore." Owen grinned an uneasy grin and noticed John's haunted face matched his own sick feeling.

"You okay? You look upset by my memories."

John returned the sick smile. The conversation with Llewelyn had confirmed his last memory of scrambling out the trench and shouting orders at his men.

"You did know the Allies eventually won, didn't you?" Owen added.

"Victorious, eh? Or the Germans simply lost before we did. Yeah, I knew that." John had devoured all printed material he could find about the battle, but the reports revealed only information about numbers and strategies. "I haven't read anything, though, by a soldier who experienced it on the ground, only generals who planned and analyzed it."

Finished with his horror story, Llewelyn's face brightened again. "In my present life, I own this butcher shop. By the way, my name is Owen Llewelyn. How can I help you, Inspector?" He held his hand out to John, and the two soldiers shook hands.

"In my present life, I'm John Ferguson from Scotland Yard, and I know who you are. Anne told me yesterday. Mrs. Winthrop, Anne Winthrop, told me yesterday. When you were taken to hospital."

"Oh, Annie, my Annie." Owen smiled thinking of her. "Isn't she something? The love of my life. I don't know if I would be sane or even still alive, you know, after the war if it wasn't for her."

John understood that more than Owen would believe.

"I became so depressed when I first got home, I actually thought about killing myself. You might find it hard to understand somebody having a hard time after making it home alive. And don't be telling this to no one neither. This stays between two old soldiers, right?"

John understood. He nodded his head. No, he wouldn't tell anyone else's tale.

"She makes my life whole somehow. We're going to be married soon. Did she tell you that yesterday? She told me you kindly walked her home last night."

"You're going to be married?" John managed to keep his voice even. "No. No, she didn't mention that."

Llewelyn waited for a question with the smile still on his face.

John tried to recover from this news which had evoked a picture of her, consumed with passion beneath him, but he couldn't remember her mentioning her engagement.

"So, did you wish to ask me some questions about Mr. Gruber's murder, Inspector?"

Llewelyn's demeanor appeared to John to be straightforward and honest.

If he knew something about John and Anne from last night, he showed no signs of it.

John collected himself. "Did you have any reason to hate Hans Gruber?"

"Absolutely none."

"You had no complaints about this rich German like—like the Germans who nearly blew your leg off?"

Llewelyn narrowed his eyes. "I have no love for the stinking Krauts. They can all go to hell. Hans lived and worked in his pawnshop my whole life. He didn't have nothing to do with my leg or the war." He thought John's idea preposterous.

John unwrapped the knife and showed it to him. "I have what we believe is the murder weapon here."

Llewelyn took the knife and examined it. "It is like ours, but none of our knives are missing."

"On the contrary." John turned to the set of matching knives behind him and next to the bloody, wooden slab where the meat Llewelyn cut up still lay. An empty slot revealed an absence of one knife in the set. John removed the murder weapon from the evidence bag and set the knife into the space. It fit. A perfect match. The right size, same brand, same degree of wear. Llewelyn tried to think of a rational explanation. He turned back to John, perplexed.

"I don't…I have no idea…" The butcher's expression turned to fear as the realization dawned on him that the fit of the murder weapon into the knife block linked him to the crime.

An older woman appeared from behind the young Llewelyn. From such a strong resemblance—probably just as handsome as Owen in her own time—John deduced she must be Owen's mother.

Gruber's housekeeper is Owen's mother.

"Owen, the truck is here. I need you to talk to Harry." She glared at John again today.

At Gruber's apartment, he had had the impression there might have been something more than a business arrangement between her and Gruber. Today, he finds the murder weapon belongs to her and her son.

"Mother, this is Inspector Ferguson. He has some questions about Gruber's murder." Owen Llewelyn had become deadly serious now. No more smile.

"Perhaps I can answer your questions, Inspector, while my son takes care of this meat delivery."

"That would be fine."

Mrs. Llewelyn maneuvered Owen toward the delivery in the back then turned to face John.

"One of your knives appears to be the murder weapon, Mrs. Llewelyn," indicating the knife block behind her.

She turned and picked out the murder weapon from the set without hesitation.

"You look surprised, Inspector. I knew which knife had gone missing. Owen would never notice such details. I suspected it might be the one used on Hans when I heard how he died and ours wasn't returned."

"You thought you knew and didn't report this to the police? Why not, Mrs. Llewelyn?"

"Because I knew you would look at us the way you are now, and we would get blamed for the murder, that's why. Yes, we own the knife, but neither my son nor I had reason to harm Gruber—an old, old friend and my employer."

John pressed her. "Perhaps you and Hans had been more than friends. Perhaps you wished to become more than friends, and he rejected you."

"That's ridiculous!"

"Then how do you explain one of your own butcher knives being the exact knife that killed your friend?"

"Why don't you ask Anne Winthrop."

Stunned, John said, "Anne? Why would I ask her about your knife?"

"Because she borrowed it the morning of the murder."

"Why would she need one of your knives?" he asked defensively.

"I didn't ask the hussy."

"Huss…hussy? Why would you call her that?"

"It's not only me that calls her that. Look at how she dresses. Red paint on her lips. And men."

"And men? What does that mean?"

"She uses them, don't she?"

"She uses men? How can you say that about the woman your son is going to marry?"

"She's pulled the wool over his eyes too, exactly like her dead husband who could never please her. Poor Peter, she drove him into joining that stupid war so he could maybe, finally, impress her. He couldn't seem to do nothing as good as Daddy. Her parents always spoilt her. She learnt how to get whatever she wanted from Daddy. And the poor man. Peter died such a horrible way. Now she has set her cap on my Owen, and he can't see what she is."

"Why would she want Owen if she didn't love him? She doesn't need a man to support her. Her chemist shop makes enough money for her family."

"Maybe there's never enough money to keep her happy. Or maybe she's a sex maniac."

"A what?"

"Sex maniac. I read about it in a magazine. They say there are some women who can't get enough, you know. Why else would she be exposing her naked legs like that, cutting off all her hair and those blood red lips?" She said with disgust. "No God-fearing woman would act that way. She certainly has bewitched my Owen. He can't see it." She stopped and thought for a moment. "You know she went back to Old Town after she came home last night. Me, sitting here watching Eddie and her invalid mother for the evening, out of the kindness of my heart, waiting for her to come and take them home, and she goes back to the partying. Can't get enough, I say."

"She went back into the walled city? That can't be right."

"I watched her go out." Mrs. Llewelyn's eyes dared John to question it. "I hadn't noticed her come home, but I saw her sneaking back up the alley in the rain towards the dancing and the men. I heard the clock in the hall strike ten. I had to wait another hour before she collected her boy and her mother."

John knew it was about ten when he had reached the hotel.

She would have had to leave almost as soon as I left her in bed, close to sleep.

Or so he thought.

"Maybe she wants him to guarantee her a good income. My Owen is working hard and even in these hard times, he keeps up our loan payment. Hans Gruber, a good man who gave fair terms to people, and he was willing to loan money to people the banks wouldn't loan to. Many people, including us I have to admit, are relieved that his death meant their debts became null and then…"

"What do you mean? Your debt became instantly paid off?"

She realized she had said too much. "Nothing. I didn't mean nothing at all."

John found that he didn't like this woman or her vicious mouth and her insinuation.

He leaned close to her face. "Tell me how you believe your debt is canceled by Gruber's death, Mrs. Llewelyn. This is a murder investigation, and you stand there holding the murder weapon."

Shocked, she laid the knife quickly on the counter in front of her as if that would absolve her of any guilt.

"Hans kept each loan in a metal box in his office at night, not in a bank vault. Everybody knew that. When you paid, he marked it down on your paper and put it back in the box right under the counter all day. Most everybody on this block owed him money. Lots of folks figured someone killed Hans to erase their debt when they got desperate enough. We hoped whoever killed him took the box and burned everybody's paper. But then, that nasty young man, Will Parker, comes slithering around. Says he found Gruber's box and is offering us a discount on our loan. Says we'll pay him or he'll sell the loan box to Gruber's son, and then we'll be back to paying the full amount."

John knew this certainly gave Will a great motive for the murder. Kill the pawnbroker, steal the loan box, and send the pub crowd in to make sure any evidence he left got destroyed. It also would explain his odd behavior, antagonizing people last night. He probably infuriated a lot of people by this scheme, that created a list of suspects in Will's murder as long as Gruber's loan list.

Mrs. Llewelyn wasn't finished. "I say either Will killed Gruber or that piece-of-work Anne Winthrop did it. She borrowed that knife the day of the murder."

Owen reappeared in the shop and screamed.

"Mother! That's nonsense! You have no good reason to dislike her. Why are you doing this?"

"Inspector Ferguson," he said, forcing himself to speak calmly, "why don't you question Will Parker? Ask him about his discounted loans."

"We discovered Will Parker dead this morning. He either fell or someone deliberately pushed him off the walkway around the top of the city wall last night."

Owen took a deep breath. "Did you find the loan box anywhere?"

An odd reaction, John thought. Not surprise, not shock, not pity in learning about Will Parker's death. His first impression of Llewelyn from sharing his war experiences turned out to be flawed to say the least. *Comrades in arms?* While Mrs. Llewelyn appeared too shocked to say anything, Owen appeared not surprised at all about Will's death.

"No, we haven't found the box. Yet. And, I need the knife back."

Owen reached back, took it from his other knives and handed it to the inspector.

"Look," Owen said, "whoever got hold of the knife from Anne must be the killer."

Mrs. Llewelyn snorted. "No one took the knife from her. She murdered him."

"Mother, stop. That's ridiculous."

"I'll have more questions for you later at the police station."

John wrapped the knife and left the butcher shop, disturbed by his encounter with this mother and son duo.

A triumphant smile grew on Mrs. Llewelyn's thin lips, knowing she had planted doubt in the inspector's mind about Anne.

Owen clenched his fists and his jaw. Out of view of the butcher shop window, John stopped.

Anne uses men? Where is Mullins? We've got to find the loan box. And I need to speak to Anne.

The conversation with Mrs. Llewelyn left John with a knot in his gut. His career would be sunk if Anne had been using him.

Could that possibly be true? He thought. Scotland Yard detectives do not get involved in any way with anyone connected to a case. Especially not sexually involved.

He had told himself that she wasn't even a witness, only a person acquainted with the deceased. There should have been no conflict.

Things change as a case develops. I have always been impeccably impersonal and professional since my first case with Alistair Howell. Oh God, Howell's face when he finds out. Howell, who believed in me when no one else did. My problem isn't about having hallucinations about the war. My problem is my image of a fantasy woman. She uses men?

He pictured the softness in her eyes. Was it all a lie? She had borrowed the murder weapon the day of the murder. Was she using him to divert suspicion from herself as a murderer?

John remembered how coldly she had reacted to Gruber's murder and how she had told him about her enslaved mother.

He spotted Mullins step out of The Swan carrying their murder bag.

"Mullins!" John turned and rushed towards him with the new information about the loan box. His brain returned to Anne while he tried to talk to Mullins.

Her rising to meet him as he kissed her breasts.

Mullins said, "Parker couldn't find a key and it didn't seem imperative to break into it right then. But, now...Maybe he stuffed the loan box in the chest."

John tried to focus but was interrupted by his thoughts again.

Her face. Her voice. That moan. Could I have misjudged her so completely?

Mullins continued. "You know the boy, Charlie? I think he knows something."

Please, God, don't let her be the murderer of Gruber...or Will Parker. Or Gruber and Will.

"Mullins, we need that damned box. Break into the chest if they can't produce a key." John handed the murder weapon to Mullins. "Put the knife in the evidence bag for now and go coax information from the boy. I need to speak to Anne Winthrop about the murder weapon."

"Anne Winthrop? What's she got to do with the knife?"

"You concentrate on finding Gruber's loan box."

"But Anne? Really?"

Ferguson knows something, Mullins thought, and he hoped he had deduced something brilliant. Mullins believed in John, his hero. He believed they were finally making progress. His step quickened toward the pawn shop.

John started for the chemist shop. He pictured Anne while they made love.

She enjoyed it, didn't she? Brazen hussy? Fiancée? Can I even look at her?

He stepped into the shop. Anne stood behind the counter helping an older woman with her purchase. Glancing up, she shot him a smile, a smile that burst in him like a bolt of electricity melting his heart. The customer felt the charged atmosphere and turned to locate the recipient.

Is this all a lie? John thought. *Am I merely haunted by a ghost encounter from over a year ago on a surreal train ride?*

He stood gritting his teeth until the woman walked past him out of the store.

Anne came to him, arms out, discreetly, at waist level.

John stepped back. "I spoke to the Llewelyns this morning. Owen seems to be alright." Anne stopped short seeing a different reaction on John's face than she had expected.

"Yes, I talked to him too."

"Congratulations on your engagement."

"Owen asked me to marry him. I haven't said yes or no yet." She frowned. "What's wrong?"

"You went out after I left you last night. In the rain. I thought you were about to fall asleep, happy and content, snug in your warm bed."

"I didn't go out. Who said that? Owen's mother, right?"

His salvation or damnation lay in her face, if he only knew how to decode it.

"My modern ideas threaten her." She started pacing, staring at and talking to the floor. "I feel more comfortable in London. Here I'm out of place. While I went to school, I met lots of women who wanted more from life." She looked at him now and spoke fervently. "The war changed the world—not solely for men. I don't want to ever depend on a man to survive. I have my own ideas. I thought you could understand that. You must know independent women in London who refuse to return to a world where only men have choices. I want choices. We proved ourselves during the war. Resourceful and strong. I can make my own choices. I have my profession and can support my family. That

Welch Dragon, Mrs. Llewelyn, and other women around here are threatened by change. I don't need any man." Anne glared at John.

"You have your profession thanks to Hans Gruber sending you through pharmacy school." He ignored the rest of her tirade.

"I don't want to end up like my mother. Forced to sleep with a man who would pay the bills. The price is too high. No one can ever make me do that. I have my license and my shop now and my mother will never be dependent on anyone again."

"Except you."

"What?"

"Your mother is an invalid. Her every moment now depends on whatever you decide."

John noticed Lisle listening from behind the curtain to the back of the shop.

Anne began to cry. "And how horrible would that be?" She became angrier. "She can't tell me what she wants. When I can pay back the loan and free her from Gruber's filthy hands, she becomes…she is…God, what a horror her life must be." She started sobbing, "My poor mother."

Lisle ran in to comfort Anne.

Anne brushed away her tears.

"I'm fine, Sweetheart. Don't you worry about anything. Go upstairs and check on Eddie for me. I need to speak to Mr. Ferguson."

Lisle left them only reluctantly, giving John a scathing look on her way out.

"You became angry last night at Will Parker because he informed you that your loan from Gruber is now money due him." John hoped her look of loathing wasn't about him.

"Will is a bad person. He hurts people. He wants Lisle. He is becoming obsessed with her, and I said he would never go out with her. He will never touch my Lisle. She is innocent and needs goodness and happiness after what she's endured. Not a criminal. A blackmailer. When I told him that, he got angry." Anne stopped. "You saw that?"

"You're not denying he discussed possessing Gruber's loan box?"

"What would be the point? You know it's true or you wouldn't say it."

"Anne, Will Parker is dead. Last night. Probably murdered."

Her face revealed nothing. No reaction and he desperately wanted a shocked or a repulsed reaction to this news. She only stared at him. This modern woman with the painted red lips blandly awaited his next question. He ached to ask her if she loved him at all, but didn't.

"Did you borrow one of the Llewelyns' butcher knives the day Gruber was murdered?"

She glanced quizzically at him. "We borrow one of their knives every once in a while. I don't know whether we borrowed one that day. Why? What are you saying, John?"

"Why did you borrow such a large knife? What did you use it for?"

"When we get big bundles of dried herbs from various farmers, the bundles are usually tied together with rope."

John walked over to the doorway leading to the back of the shop, threw back the curtain, and stepped into a small cluttered workroom between the shop and the living quarters. Scissors lay on the table with bits of snipped twine and ribbon. He grabbed a bundle of drying herbs hanging upside down from a clothesline, inspected the twine holding it, picked up the scissors, and easily cut the twine, releasing the fragrant dried flowers, which fell in a heap at his feet. Anne's perplexed, surprised expression turned to anger. Without a word, she looked around on the floor then rummaged through a rubbish bin retrieving a length of hemp rope nearly as thick as his finger that had been cleanly cut. She handed it to him.

"Cut that with the scissors."

He took the piece of rope from her which was obviously too thick for the scissors.

"We make the little bunches after we cut the rope around the larger bundles with a sharp knife. Look at my knives." She marched to a drawer in the kitchen and dumped the contents onto the kitchen table with a clatter. The drawer held several small inexpensive knives.

"Yes, we could hack away with these, but we have always gone next door to borrow one of the Llewelyns' butcher knives. But I only get bundles of herbs occasionally, so I rarely use their knives, which doesn't justify the cost of buying high-quality knives. We immediately return their knives, which I'm sure we did this time."

"The Llewelyns received a big loan from Hans to enlarge and modernize their butcher shop. With all the unemployed men these days, people eat less meat. It's been hard to repay their loan. The Welch Dragon seems capable of killing someone to me."

"Why do you call her the 'Welsh Dragon'?"

"Many people do. The Llewelyn's are originally from Wales and she's as mean as a dragon with her vicious gossip. She is a strong powerful woman, scorned by Gruber when he took up with my mother. She was in his bed then suddenly she was kicked out. Forced to watch the whole affair as his housekeeper. Since then she hasn't had a kind word to anyone about Mother or me."

Her indignation dissolved into a gentle pleading look and she stepped toward him. "John?" she said softly.

He stepped back, away from her soft voice, afraid of his response if she touched him.

"No. Not now. I need to talk to you later. Now I need to go."

Her eyes beseeched him to believe everything she said and did.

He walked out of her shop as a light mist fell from a steel grey sky, covering everything it touched with sadness. He should go to the Swan to check on Mullins's progress.

He hadn't eaten all day and felt weak and drained by the case. He headed back to the Green Man Tea Shop. His pocket watch told him he had an hour before the one o'clock reading of Gruber's will, but he had missed the observation of the Armistice.

Noon. November 11th, John realized.

The Great War had officially ended at eleven o'clock in the morning on the eleventh day of the eleventh month two years ago. He could detect nothing special that York had done in commemoration for the event, at least not on Holgate Street. Last year the whole country stopped for a moment of prayer for the dead at the exact time. No one mentioned anything special happening here tomorrow for the second anniversary. He had been either with the Llewelyns or Anne. No parade down Holgate. He would have noticed that. Probably yesterday's parade at the St. Samson's Day festivities sufficed.

He walked toward the hotel and the tea shop for a bite of lunch. Cars splashed through puddles up and down the street beside him. A wagon stood with two, white-faced, chestnut horses waited stoically while two men heaved heavy gunny sacks out. The men joked with each other. A grey-haired man and woman in front of a bookstore talked to a young boy. Apparently, taking a moment to remember the appalling sacrifice from two years ago asked too much of the people of York.

Before stepping into the Green Man Hotel, he noticed people down the street slowly enter the pub. News of the Parkers' tragedy had spread.

Why should people remember old wounds? There were always fresh ones.

John called Weems from the phone alcove in the hotel who agreed to pick him up at 12:45 and take him to Gruber's solicitor's office for the reading of the will. Then he called Superintendent Howell in London and learned that he, like most of the officers from Scotland Yard, had left the building to watch the procession of the Unknown Soldier to Westminster Abbey. He left a message saying he would call back. At least London remembered her dead.

Mullins stood at the bar in the pub, waiting for Mr. Parker, cap in his hands, the murder bag between his feet. A man and wife stepped into the quiet atmosphere from the wet outside. The husband snatched his cap off and the woman, who cradled a dish of food covered with a cloth, went to Parker, who was standing behind his bar. The three stood mute. What could be said? Several women already enfolded Mrs. Parker in a circle of concern at a table near the back. One of the women spoke to her, and she turned, but it appeared to Mullins that Mrs. Parker didn't hear what was said.

She reminds me of Ma for some reason. Her powerful arms and chapped red hands spoke of hard work just like Ma. Stoic and rather pessimistic, expecting the worst, always, so that when the worst happened it could be handled. It could be lived through. If anything ever happens to me, Ma would be devastated. She had pleaded with me to not join the police force, but there weren't a lot of jobs available to an Irishman. "We don't hire Irish." Being a copper in London is better than starving in Dublin. The thing is I love being a copper!

Mullins found solving murders exciting and rewarding. He recalled his first sight of the man drug out of the Thames, with his face slack and tortured. A case no one cared about, but it had given him a chance to become a detective, to work with the best. Then when Ferguson took an interest in him, his chance to show what he could do really began. Everyone congratulated him and he received a promotion. He loved being a detective. These murders in

York were Mullins's dream come true. Ferguson's spells scared him, but he also saw him pull himself together every time he experienced one.

"Would you like a beer, DC Mullins?" Joseph Parker wiped the bar top clean with a wet towel.

"That would be grand. Would I be out of line to ask for a sandwich maybe or something to eat?"

Far from being offended, two women jumped at the chance to do something and went into the kitchen.

He took the pint offered and took out some money.

Parker shook his head. "Just find who killed my boy."

Mullins drank his beer, ate his sandwich, and watched. Several working men sat at tables, looking both angry and bored at the same time. They wore wool pants and heavy work boots in case they were called to do a job and earn a workingman's wages. After Mullins drank a bit more, the men appeared to accept him a bit and relax around him. They were less belligerent.

"I need to get into that chest now, Mr. Parker. And Charlie watched me search the room. I think he knows where the key is. We wouldn't have to destroy the lock and all if he could be persuaded to tell us where it is."

"I'll round him up."

As Parker left his post at the bar, a woman slipped in and took over tending to customers.

One of the men in work clothes approached Mullins.

"I stood in the bar that night." His gravelly voice was respectful. "You know, the night old Gruber got hisself murdered. I saw Will run in. If you had seen his face, you'd know he had nothing to do with that. His face, red. Eyes, the size of saucers. His fear made it seem like we needed to run over there. I thought maybe we could do something.

"I came in at the back of the pack and didn't make it inside the pawnshop. I stood right outside the door. I swear to you, I saw not one person take anything out'a there. A sinister feeling poured out'a that dark place where a cold-blooded killer had just taken a man's life. That's why no one touched nothin'. We all run back to the pub as fast as we run in there. The crowd each got another pint then to calm down.

Mullins wrote the man's name in his notebook. "Abraham Killabrew."

"Did you owe Mr. Gruber any money?"

"You mean like have a loan with him? Nah. I've pawned about everything, but I got nothing he would make me a loan for. I don't even have no steady job since the war ended."

"See, that's what makes it hard for me to believe no one dared to take back what you had pawned just sitting right there and seeing as how there wasn't anyone to stop you?"

"That's the thing. I wished I'd a thought of it and so did others later on, but in that evil quiet over there…maybe the murderer was still in there. We just fled for our lives like some fiend pursued us back to the safety of the Swan."

"Thank you for your help. Would you mind letting me fingerprint you, Mr. Killabrew? Just to prove your story."

"Nah, go ahead."

Mullins quickly took out the ink pad and paper. Fingerprinted the man, wrote his name on the paper and had Mr. Killabrew sign it.

"Did someone murder poor Will?" Killabrew asked.

"We don't know for sure. Do you know any reason why someone would kill him?"

Killabrew shook his head. "That lad had a lot of ideas for getting rich, some of 'em legal and some of 'em not. But he was no big-time crook mixed up in nothin' dangerous."

They nodded to each other and Killabrew returned to his table.

Joseph Parker came back through the swinging door holding on to Charlie so he wouldn't escape.

"I ain't snitching out Will! That's his own private stuff. Let me go!"

Mullins followed Parker as he walked Charlie up the stairs holding onto his collar. Once inside the attic room, Parker said, "This is your room now, Charlie, if you want it."

Charlie's eyes lit up.

"That chest has got to be opened so's the police can figure out who killed our Will, son. If you know where the key is, you could still have the chest or it will be hacked open with an axe."

Charlie thought only a moment before he turned and felt along the outside of the door frame until he had the key, which stunned Mullins. He had searched along the bottom of drawers and under the mattress and in every nook and cranny in the room but had missed such an obvious place as a door frame to hide a key.

"You will stay and help Officer Mullins in every way you can—understand?"

Charlie nodded.

"I've got to go downstairs and see to your mother and run a pub," Parker said as he started down the narrow staircase.

After seeing its contents, Mullins understood why Joseph Parker had left before he unlocked the trunk. It held the sum total of his son's life, including a sapper for knocking people over the head, a sturdy canvas bag folded neatly, like all Will's possessions, a crowbar and other assorted tools. Mullins had confiscated similar things from burglars several times in the past. But the chest also held marbles and a little tin soldier, a river-washed mottled stone, things only a young Will would keep as treasures. At the bottom, Mullins and Charlie found another satin box like the one found under Will's bed. But this one held a light blue hair ribbon and a valentine, hand printed with lace around the edge. "To my friend Will," spelled out in a childish hand. Opening it up, the inside read, "Love, Mandy."

"Who's Mandy?" Mullins asked.

"I dunno. Oh yeah. A girl in his class at school. She's married to Tom Dunne and has two screamin' brats," Charlie said.

Mullins sorted through more photographs at the bottom of the box. Some were of the Parker family. He handed Charlie a photo depicting a cocky Charlie, at about eight years old, with his hands on his hips and a cigarette dangling from his lips.

"Very nice, Charlie, my lad. A baby punk."

"Very funny, Copper," which got him a clap on the back of the head. "Hey!"

"Respect for the law, laddie," Mullins informed him while he shuffled through the pile of photos.

He stopped suddenly. He held a picture of Lisle. The most amazing picture he had ever seen. She sat atop an ornate wooden table. Absolutely naked. She perched, back perfectly straight, on the edge of the table, her hands demurely in her lap and she looked straight into the camera somber, unsmiling as in old fashioned Victorian poses. Mullins couldn't tear his eyes from the photo. Her body looked as perfect as her face and hair. Incredibly erotic because there was no sense of flirtation, no sly knowing smile. She pulled you in and dared you to…what?

"Come on, whatcha gawking at?" Charlie grabbed the photo before Mullins could stop him. "Cor! What's this?" Charlie revealed a new admiration for his older brother as he stared at the photo of naked Lisle.

I thought Will desperate because he'd never touched her. All that Will had said and done seemed like he had become a bit obsessed about finally being with Lisle, Mullins thought.

The next photo showed Lisle just as naked, standing in front of the same heavy table, looking directly at the camera again. This time her arms were back on the table, hands flat. Nothing hidden from the lens. No sultry quality to her gaze. No hatred or anger—nothing really.

Mullins took the pile of photos. He knew Ferguson needed to see these.

Will and Lisle had a more complicated relationship than anyone imagined. He didn't want the lecherous young Charlie drooling on them either. Leering at them was wrong. It was disrespectful to Lisle. He would never admit to how aroused the photos made him, and he knew that the first picture he had seen of her sitting on the table would be secreted in his pocket and kept. He would do his duty and give Ferguson the rest.

"I know this place," Charlie piped up before Mullins took the last photo from his hands. "The place with the table, where he took the pictures. It's a church in Old Town. I used to follow him there sometimes. He uses it to stash his stuff."

"His stuff? What stuff would that be?"

Maybe a hiding place for Gruber's loan box.

Charlie realized he had said too much and looked down at his shoes.

"Take me there. Now, Charlie."

Chapter 7

*"and they'll be proud
Of glorious war that shatter'd all their pride"*

(November 11, 1920)

Mullins would have overlooked the ornate wrought iron gate. Even though it reached upwards twelve feet high, it sat unobtrusively between two medieval shops in Old Town and gave no indication of the public walkway hidden behind—lots of busy people on the street, but no one on the narrow alleyway leading to the chapel.

Charlie opened the gate and motioned to Mullins to walk in first. They followed the lane until Charlie stopped in front of a small, abandoned church tucked in behind the street buildings and made of the same cream-colored limestone as all the other buildings, surrounded by a three-foot-tall stone wall.

Charlie pushed open the dilapidated wooden gate. "This is the place. Holy Trinity. Nobody uses it anymore.

Opening the ramshackle wooden gate, they walked up the weedy slate path to the weathered front doors. Charlie pushed one of the double doors open, and entered. Muted light shone from long narrow windows onto old scarred oak pews, creating a hushed atmosphere. Their footsteps echoed on the uneven stone floor as Mullins followed Charlie up to the altar past an odd two-tiered pulpit with tight narrow stairs winding up the back.

Charlie waved one arm across himself as if he were a master of ceremonies. "There's the old table. Count on Will to talk some bird into posing for girlie pictures at the altar of a church," shaking his head in admiration for his brother.

The photographs had, indeed, been taken at the heavily scrolled oak table in the front of the church, which appeared to have been the altar.

"So Will used this church for his private business?"

Charlie looked at him unsure if he was ratting out his brother or not by showing Mullins Will's secret location.

"Show me where Will hid his stuff."

"I don't know where it is. I followed him here sometimes without him seeing me. I couldn't come in until he left so I just knew this was his place." Charlie looked around. He backed up toward the door, scared.

"Charlie, help me." Mullins was eager to move away from the table and get Charlie out of there, but he needed him first. "This might help us catch Will's murderer—if he was murdered."

Charlie stopped in his tracks and looked as if Mullins had slapped him. "I don't know. Truly I don't. I'd tell you if I did." His eyes filled with tears and looked around as if he feared a ghost might appear from the gloom. He no longer looked like a smart-mouthed punk, but a scared thirteen-year-old.

Mullins realized Charlie couldn't help him anymore. He didn't know where Will hid things in here.

"That's fine, Charlie. Thanks for your help. Go on home now and help your parents."

Charlie froze.

"Go on. I'll let you know if you can help me anymore."

Charlie bolted and didn't look back.

Mullins checked to see if the table could be moved. The heavy table didn't budge. He checked around the altar and under pews. He banged around the walls for hollow sounds. From the back of the church, he looked toward the altar and saw where a choir loft had been before being crudely removed, leaving a ledge.

Along the dark back wall, he found the stair stumps. They had been sawn off for some reason out from the wall about eight inches up to where a quite small ledge remained. The stumps of the steps bent downward, indicating someone had placed weight on them beyond the capacity of the steps.

Too close to the wall, Mullins shambled up the stumps sideways, in the pitch black, trying to find something to hang on to. Grabbing the ledge at the top, he pulled himself up the rest of the stairs. The ledge, two feet wide and ten feet long, existed as a result of the loft being inexpertly pulled down. In the pitch black, Mullins stretched himself up onto the ledge and lit a match from his pocket.

Jackpot.

A candle lay atop the shelf. Mullins lit it to inspect Will's stash. A gold and garnet necklace with a broken clasp lay where it had been casually tossed.

A couple of gold rings and a bracelet lay in the bottom of a cigar box. Then he saw the metal strongbox pushed to the back edge. Grabbing the strongbox, he blew out the candle, placed it where he had found it, and took the box down the precarious staircase.

Mullins sat on a pew near one of the long windows allowing the pale light to illuminate the contents of the box. He read loan information about people he now knew and others he didn't know. Payments were noted by amount and date and signed by whoever had made each payment.

Mullins hurried out with the box to find Ferguson.

"I had four men scouring Gruber's inventory all morning. They reported not one item missing." Chief Constable Weems informed John as they arrived at the reading of Gruber's will and were ushered into a conference room with people sitting around a large oval table waiting for them. A tiny frail man who looked to be nearly eighty stood up.

"Good afternoon, Mr. Fitzwater. This is John Ferguson from Scotland Yard."

"Glad to meet you, Mr. Ferguson. Now, would you and Mr. Weems like to sit in those chairs right there? Do you both know everyone here? This is Mr. Gruber's son David."

John nodded in acknowledgement to David Gruber, a tall, blond man about ten years John's senior. He wore a dark suit and bore the familiar York scowl.

"Mr. Gruber's housekeeper, Mrs. Llewelyn." She also scowled.

"And this is Anne Winthrop. She has been asked here to represent her mother, who is named in the will and who, I believe, is unable to attend due to her health."

The solicitor turned to Anne. "I will send a representative from our offices with a copy for your mother to inform her of the will's contents as they relate to her."

Anne didn't look at John, only at the solicitor.

John and Weems took their seats where directed as Mr. Fitzwater unfolded the document in front of him and read, "I, Hans Gruber, being of sound mind and body do bequeath my estate as follows. To my housekeeper, Estelle Llewelyn, I leave two hundred pounds, the large lace tablecloth and the new brass tea kettle. Both of which she cared for carefully and admired."

A look of anger, and perhaps disgust, flashed across Mrs. Llewelyn's face before she looked down.

"To my son David, I leave my pawnbroker shop on Holgate Street in York and the personal furnishings of the apartment. If he chooses not to stay in York, he can sell whatever he desires."

"What? That's it?" David Gruber burst out. "What happens to the rest?"

"Please, Mr. Gruber. Let me finish." The solicitor continued, "To my dear friend and beloved Ruth Thornton, I leave the proceeds of the sale of all stock, merchandise, and items being held in pawn in my shop that are not redeemed according to the terms of their pawn agreement. I also leave to Ruth Thornton the sum of my bank accounts totaling approximately five thousand pounds at the time of the writing of this will, and proceeds of each and every loan that remains outstanding at the time of my death. Original loan papers are to be found in the law offices of Fitzwater, Morgan and Trimble, who have been employed to aid Mrs. Thornton in the collection of said debts. Witnessed this day the thirteenth of January, 1920."

The will was less than a year old, having been drafted after Anne's mother had the stroke.

John looked at Anne who appeared to understand the timeline too. Gruber hadn't been using her mother at all. He had loved her and left the bulk of his wealth to her to take care of her.

David Gruber jumped up, knocking his chair backward. "But I'm his son! This is preposterous!" He stormed out of the room, nearly bowling over Mr. Fitzwater's secretary as she entered.

"Excuse me, Mr. Fitzwater, but there's an urgent phone call for Chief Constable Weems."

Weems glanced at John before excusing himself to take the call.

"Did you know your mother would inherit from Mr. Gruber?" John asked Anne in a voice he thought to be quiet. But each person in the room heard and turned to look at her.

Concentrating on her clasped, gloved hands, she answered almost in a whisper. "I knew nothing of the will until Mr. Fitzwater sent a note requesting she be here. I could not even imagine it would be so substantial."

"Hans Gruber expressly requested that the contents of his will remain secret." Fitzwater explained. "I doubt that he told Mrs. Winthrop here if he hadn't told his own son, and David Gruber certainly looked surprised to me."

John agreed with that.

"Ferguson," Weems called John out of the conference room. "Dr. Berry wants us over at the morgue. He found something."

Before leaving the room, John turned to Mr. Fitzwater. "We need to leave, but would it be possible, sir, to have someone, as soon as possible, make a list of each name who owed Mr. Gruber money and the amount owing on each loan—starting with the loans on Holgate Street?"

Mr. Fitzwater nodded. An important task for Scotland Yard needed to be done and he leapt at the chance to become the man of the hour.

"Certainly, of course. I will have someone do it immediately. And then have it rushed to the police station?"

"Yes. I need to see it as soon as possible."

"Oh, quite!" Mr. Fitzwater could hardly wait to get these people out of his office so he could aid Scotland Yard in solving Gruber's heinous murder.

"One more thing, I have been told he kept his loans in a metal box in his office," John said.

The attorney looked surprised at the idea. "Well, of course he didn't. What would happen if a fire occurred or someone got hold of that box? The original signed loan papers are kept in our vault. Perhaps he kept copies of payments made in his office. But he came in weekly and recorded all payments."

"Ah, good. That explains it then."

John made a mental note of the look of surprise on the faces around the table as he turned and left with Weems.

Their footsteps echoed as they descended the stone steps into the morgue. The naked bluish-white body of Will Parker laid on the stainless table under the pitiless glare of the overhead light bulbs. The serene features of death had no effect on John.

He dared a glance at Will's hands—they had no effect on him.

Dr. Berry turned from his work table and stepped to the opposite side. "I thought you ought to see this."

He pushed up Will's right shoulder to show them a large bruise at the base of his skull. Laying the body back down he continued, "I think someone struck Will from behind with something blunt, some kind of club that made the massive bruise back there. Probably unconscious when he went over the ledge, the impact on the sharp granite at the bottom of the wall slicing into his brain killed him. There is no way, I can see, for him to have gotten the severe blunt bruise at the base of his skill and the deep gash on his forehead both from the fall. Either he fell and landed on his front or his back but not both. Someone killed Will Parker. You now have two murders, Ferguson."

With Will's murder, John realized that the doctor had shed the York scowl and was acting more like an ally that an adversary.

"Any evidence to suggest he fought with his assailant?" John asked.

"See for yourselves." The doctor picked up an arm for inspection. "No bruised knuckles or scratches to indicate he had been in a fight with anyone."

"It looks like he was surprised from the back. Could a woman have done this?" He thought of the violent exchange between Will and Anne.

"That's a pretty good-sized bruise. It took some strength. Maybe a woman with enough motivation could have done this."

"Well, a number of people who owed Gruber money believed yesterday that they now suddenly owed Will Parker money. That gives us a compelling motive for murder."

Only the drip of water from somewhere broke the ensuing silence in the grim dank underground room.

"Will I find your name on the list of those who owed Gruber money, Dr. Berry?"

The question took him off guard for a second., "Yes, I did. Not really a substantial amount. We are going to some God-forsaken place in France called 'Aisne,' where our son is buried alongside so many others in unmarked graves. After reading in the papers about the unknown man they are burying today in Westminster Abbey, Gruber agreed to a small loan for the trip. We have tickets to go in three weeks. We were to pay in installments beginning after the first of the year."

"And you borrowed from a German? Why not a good English bank?"

"Hans was only German to those who didn't know him. He lived right here in York for most of our lives. He was not my enemy or responsible for my son dying."

"I saw you at yesterday's fete arguing with Will."

"A distasteful little punk for some years, he was quickly learning to be a first-rate criminal. Last night, he offered those of us he could find who had borrowed money from Hans a fifty-percent discount to pay him. He believed, probably correctly, that no one would divulge this to the police. I'm sure everyone felt disgusted, but we're all struggling financially right now trying to get back on our feet so fifty percent seemed better than one hundred percent. Most of Britain is struggling."

"And he possibly got the loan information from the metal box in his office after killing Hans Gruber," John said. "Why in heaven's name didn't you walk immediately over to me last night after Will confronted you? He would probably be in police custody now instead of lying here on a table in the hospital morgue."

They all looked at the corpse.

The doctor looked up with the defeated look of a man with not much left to lose. "I truly don't know, Inspector."

John stared at the metal drain in the middle of the stone floor as thoughts ran through his mind.

"Why didn't you tell me about the ether smell on Gruber's body?"

"Because other than in hospital operating rooms, the only other place to get ether is from my surgery. Yes, I lied to you. You can't get ether from a pharmacy." Dr. Berry dropped his head. "Anne Winthrop, the pharmacist, brought her little boy to the surgery on the day of Hans Gruber's murder. Lisle came too and Owen Llewelyn carried him in. My wife, Lily, remembered after you asked about the ether that the bottle of ether was missing. We used a little on Eddie while Lisle held his hand. He got a nasty gash on his abdomen running into something, and I put a couple of stitches in it. That little lad is always getting banged up or becoming especially ill."

"How do you know your next patient didn't take the ether?"

Weems stood silent but turned to stare at John.

"Eddie was my last patient."

"Doctor, don't you find it amazing you are just recalling these pertinent facts? Weren't you concerned about getting your ether back?"

"Not really. Anne is such a nice young mother, and I've known her all of her life. I've also known Owen all his life. Owen is honest as the day is long. Anne, always a bright, caring girl, has grown up to care for her mother, a war orphan, and her son all alone. We figured they grabbed it up by mistake. And she is a pharmacist, so it wouldn't be in dangerous hands. She would return the ether when she noticed it. Owen certainly wouldn't have any idea what to do with the stuff. Lily and I just forgot about it since it wasn't our only bottle."

John wondered about Owen not knowing what to do with ether. He'd been in hospital numerous times with his injuries. It was worth considering what a man might do for the woman he loved.

"And the next day a body reeking of ether didn't jog your memory?"

"The formaldehyde smell in this room made the ether smell hardly noticeable, Inspector. I'm sorry, but it's true."

John, without another word, walked out of the morgue, turning back toward the street. Weems followed.

John mulled over Dr. Berry's words about Anne.

A bright, caring girl. A nice young mother…Or did the Welsh Dragon, Mrs. Llewelyn, have it right? A user and manipulator.

"What do you make of Dr. Berry's strange memory loss?"

Weems considered the question. "I don't know if I completely believe what he said, but he sure gave Anne and Owen a means for murder. They are connected to both the butcher knife and the ether."

John and Weems stepped outside into the bright overcast day just as an ambulance clanged past directly in front of them. Constable Jones ran on foot after it.

Weems called out. "Jones! What's going on here?"

The constable stopped abruptly seeing his boss. "An accident, sir. At the end of Holgate Street. Some old woman in a wheelchair got hit by a car."

Weems and John glanced at each other before following the ambulance at trot.

At the bottom of the street two ambulance attendants knelt over Ruth Thornton sprawled unconscious near her mangled wheelchair. David Gruber watched quite near the ambulance, looking pale and frightened. John remembered David's angry face upon hearing that Ruth Thornton received the bulk of his father's inheritance from less than an hour prior at Solicitor Fitzwater's office.

"What happened here, Gruber?" John asked, grabbing the man's arm.

"I...I don't know. As I rounded the corner, her chair just shot past me and directly in front of that car."

"And you didn't accidentally push the chair in front of the car?"

"What are you saying?"

John glanced at the driver of the car that hit Mrs. Thornton. He stood in front of his sedan, helpless, staring at Mrs. Thornton's lifeless body. John released Gruber's arm and stepped over to the driver, who Weems had already started questioning.

"Did you see anyone near Mrs. Thornton, here, or perhaps see anyone push her chair toward your car?"

"For instance, that man standing over there near the wall?" John said, pointing to David Gruber.

"No. No, I didn't see anyone push her. Are you saying someone deliberately pushed her in front of my car? Is she going to be alright?" he asked, as the ambulance men raised her stretcher to the back doors. The sheet didn't cover her scuffed and bleeding face, he realized. At least for now, she wasn't dead.

One of the men glanced at Weems and shrugged. "We'll see once they get her to hospital," he told them.

Weems commanded one of his constables to question the driver. He commanded a second constable to question David Gruber. As Weems walked past John he asked, in a voice so no one else would hear, "Where's the devoted daughter?" Then he jumped in the back of the ambulance that carried Mrs. Thornton and raced up the street clanging its emergency.

But the sarcasm of Weems' remark about the "devoted daughter" struck John as vindictive. He looked up Holgate Street toward Anne's chemist shop, spotting her as she stepped out of a shop only two doors from the corner and the accident. As he watched, she looked around, confused, perhaps looking for her mother and then realizing a crowd had gathered around the scene of an accident. He wanted her to look frightened at the prospect that she might know the accident victim, but she looked curious.

John was puzzled. It didn't make sense why she would want to murder her mother. Wasn't she devoted to her? The money her mother inherited? Two popular motives. *Why isn't she reacting to the accident?*

Anne spotted John. Her eyes grew wide, once she comprehended all that the broken glass and the twisted wheelchair, still laying in the street meant, but he couldn't help wondering if she conjured the look for his benefit.

"Anne."

"My mother. I was...we were...what? How could this happen?" She walked up the street, following the ambulance.

John stepped in beside her, "How did your mother get in harm's way with no one to notice? What were you doing in the..." He glanced at the shop from where Anne emerged. The sign read "Wilson, Tailor." From the doorway, a man with a tape measure around his neck watched the commotion puzzled.

"What were you doing in the tailor's shop? How did your mother get outside?"

Anne looked up at him as they walked. "I picked Mother up on my way back from the reading of Hans' will, and I told her the wonderful news of Gruber leaving most of his fortune to her. First, she cried a little, then she seemed so excited and let me know she wanted to come with me. Two dresses are being altered by Mr. Wilson back there." She turned and pointed behind them. "He alters clothes for Mother and me because Father always bought his suits there. When I came to try them on, she wanted to sit outside in the fresh air. She so rarely feels up to going out."

John turned toward her as they continued, "Since she can't speak, how did you know she wanted to go with you and to be left outside on such a chilly day?"

"She is getting much more mobile and active all the time. She communicates a lot with us. She makes sounds and gestures with her arms and hands a little—with her whole body really. We understand her. She wanted to sit in his doorway while I went inside. Wilson's Tailor Shop has a protected doorway set back from the sidewalk, out of the cold. She smiled contentedly when I locked her chair there, and I watched her through the windows." Anne shook her head. "John, I'm positive I set the brake on her chair. She's not mobile enough to release it. What happened?"

He stopped, grabbed her shoulders, and turned her to face him. "Even if the brake accidentally released and the chair rolled onto the sidewalk, from the angle and slope of Wilson's entryway, it couldn't have made a sharp left turn and happen to roll into traffic."

"I thought she would be fine. From the back where the dressing rooms are, I could see her until I briefly went behind the curtain to try the dress on. And Mr. Wilson glanced back at her also. It could only have been a moment when neither of us could see her."

John and Anne reached the hospital. He stopped her in front of the doors and turned her toward him. "Anne, what do you think happened?"

Tears started to spill from her eyes even though he could see she fought them back. "I have no idea, Inspector Ferguson." She practically spit the words at him, then turned and went through the front door.

John felt exhausted. He needed to get some sleep—restful sleep. He needed to stop having the disturbing dreams with the falling and dying soldiers—and young policemen. He needed to talk to Lisle before Anne got to tell her version of events—which of course Lisle would swear to in order to support her mother. Everyone near the tailor's shop would need to be questioned.

Where are Mullins and Kitchen?

John walked back toward the chemist shop, but as he passed the butcher shop Mrs. Llewelyn yanked him aside and shrieked in his ear.

"She did it! Tell him, Owen! Tell him Anne tried to kill her own mother! I saw them take Mrs. Thornton in the ambulance."

With Mrs. Llewelyn continuing to hold his arm, John watched Owen try to control his mother and his anger.

"Do you hate the family so much, Mrs. Llewelyn, because Hans Gruber threw you out of his bed for Ruth Thornton?" John's own tone nearly matched Mrs. Llewelyn's and he forced himself to calm down.

For a split second, she appeared stunned before switching to a venomous expression that spoke volumes to the inspector. She released his arm and stepped quietly away from him.

John saw by Owen's expression that he knew about his mother's involvement with Gruber.

"I need facts. I need no more lies and half-truths, Mrs. Llewelyn. If you actually know something, anything, tell me. Otherwise, leave me to solve two murders."

Owen positively beamed at him for succeeding in shutting his mother's mouth.

John left the shop knowing he needed to put aside his antagonism towards the Welsh Dragon. While he longed to find the spurned ex-lover guilty of murder, he also knew she kept a shrewd, critical eye on the neighborhood and might actually tell him something he needed to know. And he had to keep in mind that the friendly fellow soldier, Owen, might turn out to be the cold-blooded killer protecting Anne.

John entered the chemist shop next door to the Llewelyns and found Lisle standing behind the counter minding the shop. She watched him warily while little Eddie played on the floor with a wooden train engine.

Upon spotting John, Eddie jumped up babbling, "Tane, tane!" He ran toward John holding the train up.

Concentrating on Lisle, John took the toy without really noticing.

"Eddie, leave Inspector Ferguson alone. Come over here."

The little boy babbled excitedly about his train.

John cupped the back of Eddie's head as he handed him back the toy.

Eddie clutched John's leg.

"Lisle, I have bad news for you. Your grandmother, *Mamie*, has been in an accident."

Her eyes got wide, "*Mamie*, no!" Only a whisper came out. "What happened to her? Where is Anne? Is she alright?" Agitated, she came around the front of the counter.

Eddie grabbed John's pant leg and babbled up at him, "Quack! Quack!"

Lisle grabbed him up as he clung to John's pant leg.

"Your *Mamie* was struck by a car, Lisle."

"Is she dead?"

"An ambulance took her to hospital. Anne is there now."

"Quack! Quack!" Eddie insisted.

"Quiet, Eddie!" She shouted at him, shaking him, and startling him into silence.

Eddie stood, pouting, his lower lip sticking out. He looked up at John accusing him of being the reason he had been yelled at.

"What does 'Quack' mean?" John said.

"Who knows. Something about a duck. We must go to her now."

Lisle scooped up Eddie, pushed John ahead of her out the door, turned the "Open" sign to "Closed" in the door's window. She walked out the door, setting the boy down only while she locked the door.

Looking up to John, Eddie implored, "Quack" once more before Lisle turned back, grabbed him up again and scurried off up the street. Eddie stared dolefully at the inspector over Lisle's shoulder as they walked up the street.

Lisle's reaction to the news had been the most emotion he had ever seen her show. She genuinely cared about her family, but he already knew that.

John looked up and down Holgate Street. The day grew colder and it started to drizzle as he walked toward the hospital. People scurried along on their errands now. An ordinary day. Nothing shrieked of the two people murdered in the last four days on this block. Or for that matter that a car had hit a woman sending her to hospital.

Odd. John thought. *Even heinous violence doesn't alter the flow of life. Four years of war, fifty thousand British men had been killed each day. Today, a brief nod to the events of the war acknowledged in Westminster Abbey, the burial of the Unknown Soldier. And then the forgetting would continue. The ripple disappeared into flow. It wasn't a studied thing. No one aimed to forget even the important events of their lives. An irresistible, unnamable law of nature requires everything to continue on. Within five years no one will remember exactly under which stone in the Abbey the poor bastard is buried. How many feet will have trod over him continuing the flow of life?*

As John neared the tailor's shop, he noticed constables, including Kitchen, questioning people on both sides of the street.

Kitchen acknowledged John with a nod.

As John entered the shop, he wondered why Kitchen hadn't gone with DC Mullins.

The tailor, a short older man, bald with a few strands of brown hair swept across his entire scalp, still wore the measuring tape around his neck and looked ill at ease standing in front of his counter.

"I'm Inspector John Ferguson. I'm from Scotland Yard and…"

"Oh my, Mrs. Thornton's accident involves Scotland Yard?" Mr. Wilson was alarmed.

"No, I'm in York because of Mr. Gruber's murder, but I did have a couple of questions to ask, if you wouldn't mind?"

"Well, I already answered the policeman's questions."

"This will only take a moment. Tell me about Mrs. Thornton's and Mrs. Winthrop's visit. Did it seem to you like Mrs. Thornton wanted to come in with Anne or stay outside?"

"Oh, Anne said it would make her mother happy and that she wished to remain outside and that we must hurry and not leave her alone too long. She takes such good care of her mother. That must be so hard for her."

"Did you see her mother's face? Do you know that she really did want to stay outside?"

The tailor looked confused.

"It seemed fairly cold even an hour ago. Did you get a sense that Anne wanted her mother left out there and ignored her mother's wish to be inside in the warmth?"

"Well, Anne said she wanted to sit in the doorway and enjoy the day. It wasn't going to take long to try on the two dresses and make sure they had been altered correctly. Why would she leave her mother outside if she wanted to come in here?"

"Did you see anyone standing around outside near Mrs. Thornton's chair? Somebody who could have pushed her down the sidewalk?"

"I don't understand why you policemen think someone would deliberately try to harm Ruth Thornton. That's ridiculous."

John looked out the glass front door. "How do you think her chair slipped out your doorway, went up and over the slope of the entryway, made a sharp left turn, and rolled to the end of the block into traffic, Mr. Wilson?"

The tailor's eyes resembled saucers as he tried to make sense of the possibility that someone wanted to hurt Mrs. Thornton. "I can't imagine, Inspector."

John left the tailor's shop a few minutes later after asking Wilson whether he had a loan with Gruber. The tailor readily admitted it but appeared baffled when John explained that Will's plan to collect on discounted loans had failed. But Wilson looked to be not terribly burdened by the news that he still owed the full amount of his insubstantial loan. John thought it highly unlikely that he had harmed anyone and would cross him off the list once the lawyer got John a copy of everyone who owed Gruber money.

John pulled his overcoat closer against the cold and crossed the street to the hotel to use the telephone. As he passed the front desk, the clerk held up the murder bag.

"Do you need this, sir? The young officer left it earlier."

John looked inside to see that the murder weapon was still present.

"Fine. I'll take care of it. Did Constable Mullins mention where he was going?"

"No, sir, but he had the young Parker lad in tow."

John figured Mullins must be still trying to locate the loan box.

From the phone booth in the foyer, John first dialed Superintendent Howell in London, who advised John that ether could not be obtained at a pharmacy store. In turn, John briefly summarized their progress on the Gruber case—or lack thereof, given that things were definitely not progressing—and informed Howell about the Will Parker murder.

John detected a tiny pause before Howell said, "Should I send more men to help with this investigation?"

If so, Howell would have made a decision without asking any other detective. The question respected their previous relationship, but it also implied a slip of Howell's confidence in John. The outcome of such a public case reflected on Scotland Yard and Howell's gamble on his returning protégé. Failure is never an option for Howell.

"Give me a couple more days to sort out some leads, sir."

"Fine, but keep me informed of your progress." Then Howell hung up.

John needed the list of those who owed Gruber money. He phoned the police station. Weems reported he had just received the list and would send it to the hotel.

"No. Is my DC and Constable Kitchen around?"

"Kitchen is here but not Mullins."

"Maybe it will be quicker, more efficient, if you have your men bring someone on that list to the station and have Kitchen ready with his fingerprinting set."

John hung up and marched to the station. He meant to scare people into giving up more information, and having a burly policeman escort one to be questioned at the police station tended to be effective. Getting fingerprinted made being questioned more threatening.

As soon as he entered the police station, even before he spoke, John's new commitment and tenacity were evident. John turned over the murder weapon to a uniformed constable who scurried to dispatch it to the evidence room. Then he was swiftly escorted to an interrogation room where someone brought him the requested tea. The list of debtors lay on the table before him. He took off his suit coat and rolled up his sleeves as he read through the names. He stopped when he got to "Chief Constable Harry Weems."

John's chest heaved. He stood, pushing his chair back, hitting the wall behind him.

As John passed by on the way to the Chief's office, Kitchen stepped out of the way. He was eager to take fingerprints.

Without knocking or waiting, John barged into Weems' office. "Why didn't you tell me you had a loan with Gruber?"

"It's not really important."

"Did you know about Will's discount scheme?"

"No. He wouldn't inform me, being the chief constable—at least not until convinced his plan worked on the other people on the list."

"What is your loan about?"

"Is that really any of your business?"

"I will eventually know the reason for the amounts loaned to each person on the list."

Weems could see it was no use refusing him information. "Mary and I borrowed some money to help our daughter and her new husband get a little house. They had some money and we added a little…"

"And you used what as collateral?"

"None. Hans said he didn't need any from me since we had known each other for years."

"Weems, what else do you know that you haven't seen fit to tell me?" John's voice rose a little.

"Nothing, Ferguson. I have no clue who killed Hans or Will."

The two men stared at each other for a few seconds. Weems added, "Look, Ferguson, I knew about him and Ruth, Anne's mother. I'd see her creep over to the shop late—after the housekeeper went home. Seemed a bit overly randy to me—slipping it to two women at a time—and no marriage nor nothing. I dunno. He wasn't who I thought I knew all those years."

"Look, Weems, we need to get on this, whether Gruber had been truly kind of sleazy or what."

Chief Constable Weems sighed and nodded.

"Next, I wish to question David Gruber. Have him brought in."

John turned and went back into the room where Kitchen waited with his ink pad and an officer who would transcribe the interviews. The first person brought in proved to have a small loan, always paid on time, an alibi for the night of Gruber's murder, and was genuinely surprised to learn of Will Parker's plan.

Next, David Gruber sat down and only when Kitchen fingerprinted him did his surliness change into wariness.

John saw him realize the time for pouting about the will had ended.

"Kitchen, I need you to take Mr. Gruber's fingerprints immediately and compare them to the ones found in Hans' pawnshop directly after the murder. You know, before David Gruber arrived in York."

David Gruber paled and watched as Kitchen rolled the last print onto the paper and eagerly took the fingerprints out of the room, leaving him and the inspector alone.

"Where is it you came in from?"

"What do you mean?" Sweat formed on David Gruber's brow.

"I mean where do you live? Did you come by train?"

"Yes, I came by train. I…I live in Winchester."

"Married? Children? What do you do for a living in Winchester, Mr. Gruber?"

"Yes. Two. A boy, thirteen, and a girl, fourteen. I am a clerk in a bank."

"And will Constable Kitchen find your fingerprints in your father's pawnshop taken at least one day before you supposedly arrived in York?"

"No! You're saying I had something to do with my own father's death. That's preposterous. Even if I had known I would get so little from the bastard's will—which I did not know—it's certainly not worth killing my father for." His voice calmed. "And I have been to the shop before. Maybe there'd still be, you know, old ones, old prints."

"You said your father's a bastard. Bastard fathers get killed by disgruntled sons all the time. Why did it take you two days to get here after his murder? Weren't you informed of his death soon after it happened?

"Yes, Weems called me that morning. You see the thing is, we never got along, my father and me. I never seemed to live up to his expectations, and I moved to Winchester after Mother died. I have a good job and a nice family and…"

"Do you understand that by pushing Mrs. Thornton in front of that car you still inherit no more from your father if she dies?"

"That is ridiculous. I…"

"Did you do that because you were angry?"

"Now listen here, Ferguson, I simply stepped around the corner as the car hit her. I didn't do anything. Why would I be standing there watching when you arrived if I were responsible?"

"Do you have your ticket showing when you arrived in York?"

"No, I don't keep old train tickets, but I arrived on the 4:03 yesterday afternoon."

"In time to find out from any of those who had loans with your father that Will offered them discount loans. Did you stop Will from taking over loans you believed you were owed by killing him?"

"That's ridiculous! I didn't speak to anyone about any loans. I have been gone for years. I didn't know who my father had loaned money to. You have no proof of any of this. You're blindly accusing me because you have no idea about any of this!"

"You may go for now."

David Gruber was right. John had flailed away at him, trying to scare up something. He would question each of the loan holders to see if they had spoken to David Gruber and when.

As the young Gruber rushed out, John noticed Mullins standing, waiting, holding a metal box and, behind him, a scared looking man and woman waiting to be interrogated next.

"Mullins. Is this Gruber's loan box?"

Mullins nodded, clutching the box as he entered the room.

Good work," he continued. "But after the reading of Gruber's will in the lawyer's office, we know that there is an official legal record of every one of his loans. That box may have some updated payment information or maybe something written by Will that might give us a clue. Did you get a chance to read any of it?"

Mullins shook his head no.

John recounted the details of the will, then the facts about Mrs. Thornton's accident.

"My God! How did she get out into traffic?"

"Well, she had asked to be left in the fresh air while Mrs. Winthrop went briefly into the tailor shop."

"Is she dead?"

"Not as of now."

"Take this list into the next room and make notations of anything found in the box—payments that haven't been recorded or maybe an extra name or anything."

"Right, sir." Mullins took the box and the list with him. The photos would have to wait.

John waved the next couple in and the rest of the afternoon the officers interrogated the people on Gruber's list. No one had spoken to David Gruber. No one had spoken of unhappiness with Hans Gruber, either as a German or a pawnbroker. Even people with loans in arrears had not had any property confiscated. Will hadn't gotten around to informing any of the people John spoke to about his scheme. No one's prints matched anything from the pawnshop.

John instructed the constables to quit calling people in for interviews and fingerprinting. At four p.m., he finished with the last equally dry interview and went to find Mullins, who was matching the fingerprints already taken.

"Mullins, anything interesting in the box?"

"Nothing sir. It seems nothing had been disturbed—no notes or anything. So I came back here to help with fingerprinting."

"Fine. We are going to break for the day, have an early supper, and work on any notes that we need to. First, I want you to go to the train station to see if, by any chance, someone remembers David Gruber on the 4:03. Probably not, but it needs done. I will meet you at the Green Man Tea Shop."

Mullins nodded, collected his notebook, and left. John packed all of the afternoon's interrogation notes into the murder bag, and as he walked out of the station, several constables came to attention as he passed.

A few minutes before five o'clock, Mullins hurried into the Green Man Hotel, shaking off the rain from a brief, sudden downpour. He was surprised to see a group of people crowding the entryway leading to the tearoom. The hotel's desk clerk stood at the back of the crowd and turned to smile at Mullins before asking with a raised eyebrow if he needed to leave the crowd to retrieve Mullins's room key.

Mullins shook his head and pointed into the tearoom.

The desk clerk stopped him as he reached the edge of the crowd at the door. "The wireless is about to come on with the news. Mr. Ferguson is inside at a table."

Searching for John, Mullins gently pushed past the people wondering what was drawing such a crowd?

People filled every table and stood along the walls. Respectfully, they watched as the owner of the tearoom finished setting up his wireless. Still rare, these new inventions drew crowds for important newscasts.

Mullins realized the crowd must be waiting for the broadcast of the Unknown Soldier's ceremony from London. The radio was encased in an oak box one foot broad by a foot and a half tall. It had a black metal front with two large black dials placed side by side and two black switches, one above and one below the dials. A significantly bigger oak speaker was placed next to the radio. Men, with their hats in their hands, watched the screen-less boxes reverently, everyone talking quietly and solemnly, as the tearoom owner turned on his set and expertly tuned into the news from London.

Mullins spotted John at a table next to the window staring out blindly. A dainty gold rimmed teacup suspended in John's hand looked oddly out of place. His depressed and dejected expression struck Mullins as he neared the table. John appeared unaware of the crowd's eagerness or the wireless owner's proud fussing.

Lighted by the setting golden sun, John 's face appeared to be slowly melting. Rivulets of rain from the brief deluge flowed down the windows and projected hauntingly across the left side of his face. For a moment, Mullins stopped and stared at the macabre image before John glanced up.

"Ah, Mullins, I was about to order before the hubbub started. Would you care to join me? It looks like our meal will be delayed by the news broadcast."

Mullins knew he would soon need to share the shameful photographs of Lisle, smoldering in his pocket. Although, he believed the pictures had nothing to do with the case.

Mullins nodded and sat down entranced by the image of John's face melting unrelentingly before rain clouds gradually obliterated the last rays of the sunset and the illusion vanished.

The newscast filled the room and all conversation stopped. A man's voice spoke.

> *This morning, soon after the symbolic eleventh hour of the eleventh day of the eleventh month marking the war's Armistice at exactly this time two years ago, the procession began. The coffin bore a steel helmet and a crusader's sword donated by the king. Next, between a double line of one hundred holders of Britain's highest honor, the Victoria Cross, lining the nave, the coffin was carried into Westminster Abbey for a short service.*
>
> *In France today, a symbolic burial of this same nature took place. Their unknown soldier was interred beneath the Arc de Triomphe.*
>
> *…The dead man who had set out without a name, a voice, or a face only a few hours before was becoming a symbol of their loved ones.*
>
> *As the coffin was carried into the Abbey there was a sense of release. Tenderness flooded into the tomb of this most mysterious individual… There was no foreign representation. The service was brief.*

The grave was dug inside the west entrance. After the casket was placed inside, the grave was filled in with a hundred sandbags of earth brought from the main battlefields and a large slab of marble was laid over it which was simply inscribed "An Unknown Warrior."

John looked dull and waxen and wholly absorbed in his memories while maintaining his distant gaze out into the gloomy darkness.

Mullins looked around. Many men and women cried softly, remembering the faces of their lost loved ones, and projecting the dignity and solemnity of the burial of the Unknown Soldier onto their dead. The wireless owner switched off his machine. People appeared to sigh collectively, awaken, and then silently depart either alone or in small groups to grieve. Dr. and Mrs. Berry among them, neither weeping, clutched each other as they left.

Mullins felt out of place in this atmosphere since the war hadn't personally touched him. The war belonged to the Englishmen. No one from Ireland that he or his mother knew had died. He had convinced her to move from Dublin because he rightly believed there would be jobs in London with so many getting killed on the battlefields. Each face reminded him of the Parkers who grieved at the other end of the block with a son only one day dead.

John stirred restlessly and motioned for a waitress. Alice came over and curtly took their order before marching off to place it without a glance at Mullins.

Mullins could tell from John's face they would not be discussing the broadcast.

"From Alice's icy reaction, I take it you and Kitchen must have abandoned Alice for the stunning Lisle last night at the dance."

Mullins nodded. *Alice would not feel so bad if she knew of the naked photographs and how badly Lisle had been used by Will.*

"What's wrong?" John asked.

"Nothing."

"Any information about David Gruber's arrival time?"

"None. Same station master from yesterday. He looked at me like I must be balmy to think he'd remember some bloke who got off an afternoon train."

"Did you learn anything else this afternoon?"

Mullins raised his eyes to meet John's, but before he could share the pictures, they were interrupted by their roast beef being plopped down, again by Alice who still didn't smile.

Mullins stared at his roast beef. If he didn't say it now, he might not get it done.

He pulled the pictures out of his pocket, all but the one he would keep, and threw them onto the center of the table.

"I found that Will Parker was a villain indeed!" It came out a little more sharply than he had intended. "These lay locked in that chest in his room."

John sat his fork and knife down and reached for the pictures. "These seem to have been taken in a church?"

Mullins couldn't tell if the photographs shocked Ferguson or not. His expression had not changed at all. He wondered if Ferguson had perhaps become jaded from the job or from the war.

"Yeah, an abandoned chapel in the Old Town. Charlie led me there. Told me Will stashed his loot there. I eventually found the loan box on an old balcony. The altar table of that church is where Lisle is posing. How could he have forced her to pose like that? She obviously completely hates the entire thing. Look at her, at her face. It would give someone who cared for her a reason to kill the bastard!" Mullins stopped himself.

John looked uneasy.

Mullins grabbed the pictures out of Ferguson's hand and dropped them face down on the tablecloth. Then he remembered his position.

"Sorry sir." he mumbled miserably.

"I wonder what game she might have been playing, or is Will really the manipulator here?" John asked as he picked up the photographs without turning them over to look at them again and slipped them into his jacket pocket.

An unsettling thought now occurred to Mullins. Lisle might be using Will. He had much to learn about being a detective.

Another thought occurred to Mullins while he mulled over the pictures he had held all afternoon. "Anne Winthrop would have killed Will if she had ever been shown one of these pictures. She's exceptionally protective of Lisle."

"Anne?"

"Don't you remember how upset Will made her at the dance?"

"Yes, I do. She told me Will had informed her he would now be discounting her loan to Gruber."

"Maybe she's lying," Mullins said. "If she already owed money, she couldn't have gotten that upset over still owing it. Maybe it had to do with Will and Lisle. What if he decided to show her one of the photographs or maybe blackmail her? Leave him and Lisle alone or he'll spread the pictures around—something like that. Maybe she became outraged over that and decided to kill him."

The stunned pause made Mullins worry about his logic.

"But I walked her home. You remember we left before you and Tom and Lisle?"

"She could have gone back to the Old Town to look for Will after you left her. Maybe someone saw her."

John stared at him a second remembering Mrs. Llewelyn's comments, then picked up his silverware and resumed eating. "We'll question her again tomorrow, Mullins. This evening we ought to retire to our rooms, and maybe write up our notes instead of going back to the station. We can finish questioning the people on Gruber's list tomorrow."

Mullins nodded and thought John looked exhausted. But he had caused him to think about some things and hoped his deductions had impressed him.

As they walked up the stairs to their rooms, Mullins hoped Ferguson would never find out about his feelings for a woman involved in their case. *Good detectives always remain detached—always. Ferguson would be appalled if he knew.*

A loud, insistent knocking startled John. He set his pen down and answered his door. Dr. Berry rushed in.

"Ferguson, you've got to come with me right now. Mrs. Thornton has regained consciousness. She is dreadfully agitated, says she wants to speak to you immediately. Well, anyway, she got her message across that it's you she wants to see. Maybe she can tell us who pushed her into traffic."

John stepped across the hall and knocked on Mullins's door, informing him of Dr. Berry's news. Stepping back to his room, he grabbed his overcoat.

Both men quickly followed Dr. Berry. The cold rain now poured down, and all three of them pulled the collars of their coats closer and, heads down, rushed toward the hospital.

But Dr. Berry turned, instead, toward his surgery. "She's been entrusted into my care."

They entered the house through the back of the office, and Dr. Berry stopped to take off his wet coat.

"Where is she?" John brusquely asked the doctor.

"Upstairs," he said, taking one arm out of his coat.

A piercing woman's scream came from somewhere above their heads, causing the hair on the back of John's neck to stand up, then came a dull thud and a crashing sound. He bounded up the stairs three at a time, his coat still half on dragging on the stairs. Mullins followed with the doctor trailing them.

John rushed into the only open and lit room at the top of the stairs. Mrs. Berry knelt beside Mrs. Thornton sprawled on the floor next to her bed, eyes closed with a pillow still half over her face. The dark window gaped open, rain poured in, and the wet curtain drooped where it had been pulled to the outside as the person escaped. He crossed the room to the window.

Mrs. Berry shrieked, "Someone was hunched over her as I entered the room! They scrambled out the window onto the fire escape as I turned on the light." She pointed to the open window.

"Did you recognize them?" John peered into the blackness through the rain.

"I couldn't see. Only the back of their hooded raincoat."

Leaning out over the window sill, John saw a figure darting down the alley.

"Mullins, handle this," John called over his shoulder, as he stepped out in pursuit putting his coat back on, hoping Mullins would know what needed doing. Then he half climbed, half fell down a rusty, slick fire escape. The bottom four feet of the ladder, missing. He jumped into a puddle of water landing on all fours. Sprinting to the corner where two dark alleys intersected, he squinted into the blackness behind the butcher shop and the chemist shop, the rain beating into his face. He trotted ahead, looking frantically left and right, trying to spot a figure hiding behind a trash bin or in a doorway. He hoped Mullins would think to call the police station because catching this man would be hopeless without more men.

Then John spotted a yellow sliver of light. He ran to it. Someone's back door left ajar. He looked on to the far end of the alley. The blackness became only a little lighter as it got to the street at the far end of the alley. Nothing moved. Only the rain pounding against the buildings and pinging off the metal bins could be heard—except for his own breathing. The open door being a possible escape route, he pushed it lightly. He saw no one, heard nothing, and stepped into the dry, dimly lit room, easing the door shut behind him. He stood barely breathing. Listening. He heard only the dripping of raindrops from his coat onto the floor.

"Hello..." he started to call out and stopped abruptly.

He recognized this room. Anne's kitchen. A dim light shone down from the top of the stairway. He took the two steps up to the landing and looked up the stairs.

"Anne?" No sound. He slowly climbed the stairs. As he rounded the corner at the top, Anne stepped from a room wearing a robe and wrapping a towel around her hair.

"Anne," he repeated quietly.

"Oh! John, you scared the life out of me. What in the world are you doing here?" She looked genuinely surprised—to his relief.

"Come here," he said gruffly.

She walked over and stood in front of him. He pulled the towel from her head and felt her hair. Wet.

"What is it? What's wrong?" she asked.

He loosened the belt of her robe and opened it, moving his hand across her bare shoulder.

She didn't move away. She only looked up into his eyes. "What do you want, John?"

As he moved his hand along her naked side, she held her robe to the other side but made no protest. She looked into his eyes. Her own eyes half closed.

"Anne, why are you all wet?"

She blinked at him, not expecting the question. "I just took a bath and washed my hair." Her voice, inviting. She could be telling the truth or she could be wet from running in the rain. She dropped her robe and it pooled around her feet.

"What do you want, John?" she repeated putting her arms out towards him. Standing there, she looked warm and enticing with her shining clean skin, while looking innocent and vulnerable at the same time. He wanted to take her more than anything he could remember wanting, and yet he turned away trying to maintain his concentration. He thought of her mother sprawled on the floor, maybe dead, and took a step back down the stairs.

"Where is your coat, Anne?"

Anne stared at him for a moment, then bent picked up her robe pulling it back on and cinched it tight. Her face hardened against him.

Probably forever, he thought.

"Anne, where is your coat?"

"On a hook downstairs by the back door."

John turned and went back down stairs with Anne following him. He found a couple of coats on hooks by the door. One small brown wool coat, obviously belonging to Eddie, and a tan trench coat. Both coats were dry.

"That's my coat," she said.

John looked around the room for any other coats. Pushing aside the curtain that divided the back rooms from the shop, he stepped into a room lit only from the street lamp outside. The herbs and soaps smelled of goodness and cleanness. He groped for the light switch, turning a glaring brightness onto the scene. He looked around, stepped behind the counter, and inspected the shelves. Satisfied, he hurried back upstairs leaving a confused Anne to switch off the light and follow him.

John entered her room turning on the light and searched it briefly. The bed had not been turned down. Finding no wet coat, he crossed to the room she had come out of. He found himself in the bathroom and touched the tub which had recently had water in it. He sighed in relief, but his brain sent him a picture of her fleeing her pursuer and quickly running water enough to look like a bath had been taken to hide the fact that she was soaked from the rain.

John found no place to stash a wet coat here, so he stepped out into the hall and pushed open the next door. Anne's mother's room, neatly made up, awaiting her return. On the dresser was a picture of the family with a young Mrs. Thornton standing next to what appeared to be Anne's father, a young

Anne standing between them with a large bow in her hair. He checked the closet and under the bed.

Stepping out into the hallway, he entered the remaining room and turned on the light. Lisle slept in a long narrow bed with her pillow held over her ears. He wondered if perhaps that was a habit from the noise of dropping bombs. The pictures Mullins had shown him flashed through his head.

Eddie, mouth open, slept in a small bed against the far wall. Neither of them awoke. He searched rapidly and stepped quietly back into the hall. As he walked past Anne's room, he saw her sitting slumped on the edge of her bed clutching her robe.

"Anne, your mother regained consciousness. She sent for me a little while ago to tell me something."

Anne looked up at him with no expression.

He went on, "She was attacked right before I got there and was not able to talk."

Fear lit up her face. "Is she...alive?"

Fear concerning her mother's welfare or fear of being discovered, he wondered.

"I don't know."

"We must get to Dr. Berry's to check on her." She went to the closet and grabbed a dress.

John's eyes played around the room again.

"How did you know she had been moved to the doctor's house and was no longer in hospital?"

She stopped buttoning the dress for a second and sat down on the bed to put on stockings. She looked at him.

"I assumed that she would have been moved there since she is obviously recovering."

Eddie stepped into the room blinking from the light. "Mummy crying," he whined.

She lifted him up, "No, Darling, Mummy's not crying. I'm fine. I need you to go back to bed. Inspector Ferguson and I need to go see Grandmama right now." She set him back down and hurriedly finished getting dressed.

Eddie looked at John and tugged at his coat hem. "Mummy. Quack. I scared, Ferson."

Anne took her son's hand and led him back toward his room. "Don't be scared, Darling, Lisle is here. I'll be right back. Go back to bed like a good boy."

But Eddie looked behind him into John's eyes. "I'm scared," he said in a small voice before disappearing into his dark bedroom.

When Anne emerged from Eddie's room, John asked, "What is he trying to say? What is 'Quack'?"

"I don't know. I haven't heard that word before. Why?"

"He said that to me earlier today. 'Quack.'"

"Let's hurry please," she said as she started down the stairs. They reached the bottom and she turned to go out the front of the shop.

"Why don't we go out through the alleyway?"

"Well, all right, but it's always dark back there."

John opened the door for both of them and stepped into the face of a startled constable standing there, water pouring off his face, his hat, and the torch he carried.

"Sorry, sir." The constable raised his voice to be heard above the downpour. He spat rainwater as he spoke. "We're searching the alley and the nearby streets since you didn't return immediately. Did you find anyone?" He looked at Anne suspiciously.

"No. And you?" John yelled back.

"Well sir, we just got here. Wondering whether you were alright."

"I'm fine. I don't think anything can be found until morning light. Why don't we call off the search until then? Then this alley needs to be thoroughly searched."

"Right, sir."

John led Anne out of the dark alley following the constable's torch. They entered Dr. Berry's surgery, shrugged off their wet coats, and went upstairs.

"Wait out here, Anne." John went into Mrs. Thornton's room and closed the door before she had time to protest.

Anne's mother lay motionless on the bed, eyes closed with a death-like pallor to her skin. He glanced around at the doctor, Mrs. Berry, and Mullins standing close by.

Weems quietly stepped into the room a moment later. "The constable told me you came out of Mrs. Winthrop's back door."

"Yes. I found the door to her shop slightly ajar, and I entered to see if possibly the person ran in there."

"What did you find?"

"Nothing."

Mullins turned to John and held out a medium-sized brass button.

"Mrs. Thornton clutched this in her hand. I think she must have pulled it off of her attacker's coat."

John examined the button. Black thread and a bit of dark red torn cloth hung from it.

"Did she say anything?"

They all shook their heads.

"Mrs. Berry, can you describe her attacker?"

"No, I'm sorry. It terrified me seeing someone climbing out the window. I saw a dark red wool coat with a hood, and I only saw that for a second before you rushed into the room."

"Did either of you telephone Mrs. Winthrop or see her earlier and mention that her mother had been moved here in your care?"

Dr. Berry said, "No. We thought we would tell her in the morning. Dr. Connors told me they had done all they could stabilizing her, and she regained consciousness, so she needed time to mend and would do fine in our care. I think she is recovering quite nicely. As soon as she came round, she became quite agitated. Her language skills are improving marvelously. She created a sign on her chest with her hands. We figured out it was a badge and she wanted to talk to you, to tell you something. She wouldn't speak to us. She was determined to wait until you got here."

John asked, "So how is she doing? Is she going to live? She doesn't look very good right now."

"It's hard to say, but this lady is obviously a fighter," the doctor said.

"DC Mullins, would you go and ask the constable standing outside to stand guard in this room tonight?" John said. "Good thinking, calling the station and getting help, Mullins."

Mullins brightened a bit as he turned and left the room. Then he reappeared.

"Ah, Mrs. Winthrop is out here."

John said to everyone in the room, "No one is to enter this room until I get back in the morning." And then to Mullins, "Mrs. Winthrop will have to leave. Please see she gets home and have an officer see she stays home."

They left John in the room, and the young constable who had escorted them to Dr. Berry's came in looking much drier than he had when they entered the doctor's surgery. He squared his shoulders and looked at John awaiting his assignment.

"Stay inside this room and allow no one in except Doctor or Mrs. Berry and only if Mrs. Thornton's condition requires you to call one of them in. Understand?"

The constable nodded and looked eager to do as he was ordered.

John believed he was gaining more respect now because the York policemen and the Berrys imagine he is making progress towards solving the baffling case. In reality, not much more progress had been made.

The young constable in uniform reminded John of his sergeant at the Somme. Like the young man, Tipper was an eager young man in uniform awaiting his orders. John remembered. His sergeant's face, lit by the predawn exploding shells, loomed before him, trying to understand what John was screaming over the deafening noise, confident that John could save them again. He remembered their orders to retreat, abandoning all their equipment. His young soldiers, scrambling for guns, ammunition, helmets and boots. They looked scared in the flashes of light, but they looked to him with such trust. He always led them safely from catastrophe, and he would lead them now out of one more hellish fight. John found himself standing alone in Dr. Berry's upstairs corridor, he could not recall what had happened. He now knew the army safely retreated, but had all his men been killed? He couldn't remember any more.

Feeling alone and terrified, he descended the stairs back to the bottom floor of Dr. Berry's surgery. Mullins was ushering Anne out into the cold, black rain. He ached to call out to her, but she couldn't help him with his memories, or lack of them. She couldn't help him with his flashbacks.

What an absurd idea.

"See that Mrs. Winthrop gets home."

Chapter 8

"Men who went out to battle, grim and glad"

(November 12, 1920)

John awoke abruptly recalling only remnants of the end to the dream that had recurred nightly since he came to York. This night, young soldiers' heads splattered over the sidewalk, rivers of blood all round and each head, whether surprised, angry, or sad, mutely accused him of being responsible.

From his bed, in the dim early morning light, he could barely make out the furniture in his room. He listened to the gentle rain softly tapping the window panes—no longer the pounding rain of last night.

Then he knew. Straightaway. The dream had been leading him to the awful truth. The horrendous incident that he could never before face. Not his whole squad, only his sergeant, Benjamin Tipper.

He had grown quite close to this special lad in the year they spent together. Tipper was nearly twenty by the time of the Somme and a sergeant for no other reason than the scarcity of men. Smart and likable, officers and soldiers were drawn to him. Tipper kept the unit's spirits up. In spite of the war, his youthful exuberance shone. Of course, the war in some ways had ground him down too and a part of him would always be scarred by it. But it hadn't, to that point, destroyed him. Maybe the truth of why he drew others to want to be around him was simply that he wasn't grim or dead inside.

As John lay in bed, listening to the rain, he remembered.

Tipper's terror the first time the Germans shelled their unit and how Tipper looked to him for support and as an example of how to be a good soldier. The lad had become convinced, after a number of onslaughts together, that they remained alive because of John's skill and cunning.

And my wretched ego allowed that nonsense. Anyone should know after being shot at a couple of times that you live or die by sheer dumb luck.

But Tipper never saw it that way. He idolized Captain Ferguson. And John felt ashamed now for allowing such stupidity to continue and wished he didn't have to face the consequences. For so long he had struggled to remember what had happened. But as the rain grew heavier outside his window, he couldn't stanch the flow of his memory.

It had happened at the Somme. The second battle that had been fought there. This one, in March of 1918, only a few months before the end of the war. The German plan had been a massive offensive to try and destroy the Allied forces and crush their will.

The battle started before dawn. The deafening barrage from the big German guns woke John. His cot and the trenches shook from the concussions. Fear engulfed him…the trench would cave in, the falling dirt would entomb him and suffocate him in his bunk. John scrambled outside briefly disoriented by moments of light from explosions followed by a second of darkness. He tried to gather his men, but the noise made it impossible to give an order over the barrage. He yelled into Tipper's ear. The men careened around yelling at whoever they could grab while the ground heaved and buckled under their feet as huge shells exploded everywhere.

The entire Fifth Army, thousands of men, had been ordered to retreat and regroup. Thousands of men grabbed any equipment they could carry to turn and fight later when the next order came. Around the pitching, twisting ground, and against unimaginable noise, the soldiers managed to make an orderly retreat.

By afternoon, John's men dragged down a dusty road ever farther from the cannons. Tipper told stories and jokes to keep everyone's spirits up as they plodded along hoping the commander's order would be given to stop and rest. John laughed at a joke of Tipper's, or maybe John had made the joke. He could only remember they smiled at each other.

And then Tipper had no head.

Just like that. Blown clear away. His uniform stood there for a moment and then dropped like it didn't contain a man's body inside. John heard no shells explode nor men's screams nor saw any part of the landscape. He saw only Sergeant Tipper's lifeless body as it fell next to the road. The lad's hands stuck out of the sleeves—Tipper's familiar hands, thin expressive hands, dirty now but unmarred. Then a round pool of red, glistening blood grew from the body, edging toward his own boots. And that's when he had had enough of the war, enough of life. "NO," he screamed over and over. Then he must have fainted or blacked out. There was only dark nothingness.

Nothing more existed to be remembered. So much promise had died with Tipper. It shouldn't have happened. Not then, anyway, as the sun smiled down and they all laughed, relaxed. One died in the horror of the trenches—no-man's land—scrambling across a field while men shot at them. The awful, terrible, unacceptable thing about this death was that he had let Tipper down. John failed to get him safely out of the war and on with the rest of his promising life.

John, aware of the comfort of his bed, the rain slowed to a trickle, knew the dream was gone. He remembered the reality.

They're gone—forever. I know

The half-world of his existence since hospital was gone. Forever, he would see Tipper's face believing in him and knowing he had failed. He had a long road before he could be normal, but he would never need to be hospitalized again.

He snatched up his robe and bolted down the hallway to the loo vomiting until he was too weak to vomit anymore. Then he sat on the floor and held the porcelain bowl. And wept. He understood now the reason for his discomfort with Mullins' hero worship. And Kitchen's. He couldn't be anyone's hero. Such notions were not only ridiculous, they were also dangerous. Seeing Will Parker's lifeless hands in the morgue had triggered the memory of Tipper's hand, protruding from the headless soldier's sleeve on the battlefield. John washed up and went back to his morning-lighted room. He wished he could forget why he was here in York. But he knew he had work to do. He got dressed, then sat on the corner of his bed, staring blindly at the rug until Mullins knocked on his door and they went down to breakfast.

Stopping first at Dr. Berry's surgery, Mrs. Berry led them up to Mrs. Thornton's room.

John asked, "How is she?"

"Better than we expected, but she is still unable to communicate much."

They entered the room and saw her now sleeping.

Dr. Berry came into the room. "She needs her rest. Come by this afternoon. She might be recovered enough to talk about what she wanted to tell you."

When John and Mullins reached the police station, they found Weems ordering men off on various errands. He greeted the men excitedly.

"Ferguson, I've arrested Anne Winthrop for the assault on her mother. I sent some lads over early this morning to shake up her place and see if they could find a coat that matched the button her poor mother was clutching. I knew you were on the right track last night, and they found it. A red jacket missing one matching brass button stuffed behind the counter of her shop. Good job."

Perfect, thought John.

Weems continued, "Anne's mother must have known something about Hans Gruber's murder, or Will Parker's. Anne realized her mother could better communicate and had become a threat. She must have thought suffocating her mother would tie up a loose end."

"Have you questioned her yet?"

"Once we showed her what we found, she hasn't spoken a word. She's downstairs in a cell. I thought maybe you should have a go at her."

"Right. Mullins, go question Lisle first thing about the photographs. Find out if Anne had seen them. If she had, that would be a strong motive for murdering Will Parker. And, Mullins, find Kitchen and take him with you to talk to Lisle.'"

John turned and followed Weems to the cells.

With mixed emotions about his assignment, Mullins nodded and watched his two superiors leave. John's trust in him to interview Lisle thrilled him, and the prospect of seeing her and talking to her was exhilarating. Yet discussing the photographs with her troubled him. He had no intention of taking Kitchen along to become one more person who knew of the photos' existence. He turned and left the station.

John descended into a damp cellar that housed the station's holding cells. The grey stone walls radiated cold as John and Weems passed empty cells before stopping in front of the one holding Anne Winthrop. She sat on a cot in the gloomy, dank cold, facing the opposite wall, arms wrapped around herself for warmth.

"Would you like another blanket to keep you warm?"

She didn't answer.

John stared at her back and felt the same tenderness for her that he had known from the first night he met her on the train.

Why do I refuse to abandon my feelings? She has become the survivor that I had imagined she would. She refused to go down when her old world sank. She made me feel like I wanted to survive. But did her survival come at a cost of murdering two men and attempting to murder her own mother? Something still doesn't feel right. Have I become beguiled by characteristics I had invented for her?

He pictured the hacked corpse of Hans Gruber.

Can she hate that much for her mother's sake and later attempt to kill her mother when threatened with discovery? Did she also kill Will? Over a loan? Her shop appears prosperous. What reason would she then have to murder him. The photographs of Lisle, maybe. Mullins had said he thought she was so protective of Lisle she might kill anyone who exploited her. Could she possibly kill her own mother to keep her quiet about something. But what?

What about Lisle? Maybe Lisle killed to protect the world from knowing about the photographs. Then why would she have allowed them to be taken? Perhaps Gruber knew about them. But why kill Grandma? Her mamie? Maybe Owen Llewelyn killed Gruber to protect his beloved Anne. But he could have protected her without murder. Could he have killed Will for fear he might steal away her heart? Maybe the war convinced him violence was the answer to a problem.

John knew many others had a motive to kill Hans—money owed to him and feelings of his unfair treatment when they suffered during hard economic times. A German with the audacity to prosper in England with so much pain and hatred after the war. But why kill Will? The same motive? People who couldn't pay now owed it to him. One killer? Two? Same motive or different?

John looked at Anne again. What doesn't add up?

"Anne, the coat found in your house had a missing button matching the one your mother clutched from her assailant last night. Is that your coat?"

She only stared straight ahead.

"Help me out. Explain this to me so I can help you. Trust me. I want to help you."

She slowly turned to face him, haunted eyes, red from crying or lack of sleep.

"You? Trust you? You're the one who burst into my home last night and searched it. You led the police to me. Did you see that coat when you searched my house? Apparently, someone stashed it there."

"Are you saying the coat is not yours?"

She said nothing.

"Explain it. Whose coat is it? Did you try and murder your mother last night?"

She refused to say anything more.

He left her.

When he came back upstairs, Weems came out of his office.

"Ferguson, I think we have Anne Winthrop for the attempted murder of her mother, but nothing concrete on the murders of Gruber or Will Parker. Why would she kill Gruber? and Parker? We need to dig for motive—and find some evidence."

John moved into Weems' office and sat. Then he said to Weems, "We need to keep looking for other possible suspects. An obvious motive for Gruber's murder is money. We need to continue to question the loan-holders. It would help to have your men working on who did business with Gruber that day."

John read Weems' raised eyebrows.

"My men have made a list. We can start questioning them. Here's a copy of the list." Weems handed it to Ferguson. "I also scheduled Gruber's son to be interviewed this morning about exactly why he was at the corner of Ruth Thornton's accident yesterday. I was going to cancel that since…"

"Don't cancel it," John said.

"Would you like to be here when I question him?"

"Yes, I might have a few questions for him myself." John looked over the list of debtors. Estelle Llewelyn's name jumped out. "Estelle Llewelyn, the housekeeper. Jilted lover. Owen's mother protecting her son from the grasping hussy. I think I'll go ask her a couple of questions and then I'll be back for David Gruber's questioning."

Kitchen stopped John as he left the police station.

"While we searched for the jacket before Anne was arrested, people congregated at the door to the chemist shop—maybe someone slipped inside with that jacket. The scene was hardly secure."

As he walked closer, Mullins saw Lisle through the pharmacist store's front window hunched over Eddie with her back to him. He tapped the window. Lisle whirled, freeing Eddie from the wash cloth she held. Eddie scurried away from her, huddled in a corner looking at Mullins, wide-eyed, and indignantly wiped his mouth. Mullins noticed worry in Lisle's eyes and longed to reassure her that she had nothing to fear from him. He smiled and Lisle's gaze returned to her usual serene expression.

"What are you two doing this morning?" he asked.

Her face softened as she looked over at Eddie while he babbled and wiped its shiny clean redness again.

"Lisle, I have to ask you some questions. They are nothing to worry about." He tried to sound casual. Her shoulders relaxed a bit.

"Patrick." She whispered his name. The first time she had spoken his first name. Her eyes rimmed with fear pleaded with him.

He wanted to crush her to him. "It's alright, Lisle. We need some more information to help us solve these murders. Perhaps you can help us. Maybe something that you know will help Anne." Although he doubted it, he thought that might be the right track to get her to lower her defenses.

His heart skipped a beat and he stepped back when he saw the brief display of hatred on her face before it turned innocent again. "No, we don't think Anne did anything wrong, Lisle, but we need to figure out who did so we can free her. Will you help me?"

Wariness grew on her face.

"Yes, Mullins, I want more than anything to save Anne." She truly looked wretched at the thought of not having Anne nearby. "What do you want me to say?"

"I only want you to answer my questions truthfully." Mullins cleared his throat. "Last night when your...er...'maymah' got attacked, was Mrs. Winthrop, Anne, with you all the time?"

Lisle's distrust turned to confusion. "What is 'maymah'?"

"You know. How do you say 'grandmother'?"

"Oh, you mean *mamie*. That is French for grandmother."

"Okay, *mamie*. Well, did you actually see Anne? Was she home? Did she come in later? Did she come in wet from the rain?"

"Anne and Eddie and I were home all evening. No one went out. We had no reason to get wet from all that rain."

"She didn't go to see her mother at Dr. Berry's? Perhaps earlier in the evening? Maybe before supper?"

"No, we were here. We went nowhere, only home."

"And the red jacket. Is it Anne's?"

She only looked at him.

"Is it Anne's jacket, Lisle?"

"No, it's mine."

That's what he feared she would say.

"Then why didn't you tell Chief Constable Weems that earlier when he came and arrested her?"

She looked around confused. "They arrested her because of my jacket? I didn't know, but the jacket is mine. I will tell them. Let's go tell the *gendarmes* now." She pressed herself against him, holding his arm and looking up into his eyes.

He stood still, looking down into her luminous face.

"If you tell the police that the red coat is yours, they will release Anne, but they will arrest you. That would make Anne terribly sad if they arrested you instead of her."

"But what can I do then? I must save her. She didn't kill anyone."

Reluctantly, he stepped away from her and pretended to write in his notebook. He needed time to think. They didn't need two people swearing to ownership of the coat. He tried to think of a question that would make her admit that the jacket belonged to Anne, but he couldn't think of anything. He returned to the real reason he needed to question Lisle. The pictures in his coat pocket. He took a deep breath, working up the courage to question her about them.

"Lisle, did Will ever threaten you in any way?"

She turned away as if to stop even the thought of Will Parker from touching her. "No. Why do you ask me that? Threaten me? How could he threaten me? Why?"

Mullins had his opening. He took another deep breath and reached into his pocket. "I found these pictures in Will's things." He held out a couple of the pictures.

Lisle forgot immediately about the jacket and Anne. She stiffened and flashed a look at him that startled him with its fierceness. Then she calmed.

"Have you shown these to Anne? Does she know of them?"

"Why did you let Will take these pictures?"

She stared at him like a bug she wished to squash—with utter contempt.

Mullins felt the contempt, the hate.

Lisle started to open the door then whirled on him and demanded again, "Does Anne know about them?"

"No." He didn't like this transformation from her helpless need for his help to this belligerence, but he refused to back down. "But she might have to if you don't explain them to me."

"Come, Eddie, we will go to see Mummy."

Eddie didn't move from his corner.

"Come with me now!" Lisle shouted at him.

Eddie turned his face away from the noise.

She strode over to him and smacked the back of his head.

He stiffened and put his hand over his head where she had hit him.

Lisle left the doorway and walked to the dividing curtain. She pushed it aside and disappeared into the little workroom. She quickly slid a knife sitting on the table into her purse and emerged, holding the purse up for Mullins to see without looking at him. Then she bent and picked Eddie up, locking the door behind them. She marched off down the street with Eddie looking back at him.

"You can't run from my questions, Lisle," he said, trotting up to her.

John noticed Mullins and Lisle leave the pharmacist shop as he opened the door to the butcher shop. He observed Mullins was speaking seriously to her and wondered where they were going before he stepped into Llewellyn's.

From behind the counter, the Welch Dragon beamed like a Cheshire cat.

She knows about Anne's arrest, John thought.

"Good morning, Detective Ferguson," she purred.

He nodded.

"Mother, I'm—Oh, Ferguson," Owen said as he entered the storefront, slipping one arm into his jacket sleeve, revealing a large knife as his hand pushed through the other end. His face appeared grim and determined.

"Where are you going so early this morning, and what are you planning to do with the knife?" John asked firmly.

Owen looked at the knife and set it on the counter. "You can't really believe Anne hurt anybody. This is some kind of mistake. It has to be settled."

"Couldn't hurt anyone?" said the Dragon. "What about all the cuts and scrapes and stitches on that poor little boy? Who did that?" she demanded.

John thought about Dr. Berry telling him of all the times he had patched up Eddie.

"What are you talking about, Mother? You know he's simply a rambunctious little boy. Why do you come up with stuff like that?"

"Do you believe that, Inspector? You've seen more family violence than my poor Owen here. Do you believe that Eddie has more than his share of accidents? Owen has even taken Eddie to Dr. Berry's several times. And the little dear gets more frightened all the time. I would swear he was afraid to go home the other night."

Owen stared at the knife. His hand clenched and unclenched.

John asked, "What is the knife for, Owen? Where were you going with it?"

Owen shook his head, looking from his mother to John and back to his mother. Then he crumpled onto a stool behind the counter. "I don't know, but something's got to be done about Anne sitting in jail. You're wrong.

You're all wrong about her. She's a good woman. This has got to stop." His words were intended for more than John and his mother. He implored the world in general to listen to reason.

"And the knife? How could that help Anne?"

As if he had just seen the knife, Owen gave it a close look and sighed. "I don't know. I don't think I would have left with it. What could I do with it anyway?" He looked to his mother for support.

"Inspector, he's frustrated that's all. The knife simply lay near to hand. He couldn't harm anyone. Would he storm the police station wielding a butcher knife?"

"Not only did you clean the house of the man who no longer wanted you in his bed, you also made loan payments to him, Mrs. Llewelyn?"

"What?"

It pleased John that he succeeded in surprising her.

"You were one of the last people to see Hans Gruber alive. And you locked up his pawnshop at seven. You have been paying money to a man who spurned you, a German like the ones who wounded your son. The pressure of having your son involved with the people Gruber cared for might have simply been too much to take anymore. What happened when you went to make your loan payment? Did you go in with hate and did he laugh at you? Maybe I can find someone who heard you shouting at him."

She vibrated with hatred and frustration. Her face reddened and tears ran down her face. John had finally pushed her to a place where he might learn something substantial.

"All right. I told that bastard what I thought about him. He used me. I went meekly every week and paid a man who smirked at me. I hated him. He taunted me with his attitude and that day he gloated about my Owen and the little tart. He said, 'Well, it looks like your boy is smitten with Anne. Maybe a wedding soon, eh?' I would have liked to have killed him before I left for the night, but I didn't."

"You have admitted already that one of your knives killed him. I need the clothes you wore that day."

She started to wail, crying loudly, rocking back and forth, murmuring, "No, no."

Owen's neck veins bulged as he strained to control a desire to stop John talking this way, threatening both Anne and his mother. His hand now covered the butcher knife and the look on his face said he was capable of murder.

John had wanted to provoke them both and succeeded.

"Were you both at Anne's chemist shop this morning? Watching as she got arrested."

Estelle Llewelyn suddenly recovered and stopped wailing. Mother and son looked at each other.

"I think you were. I think maybe one of you planted the jacket in the confusion of the search to make Anne look guilty."

John and Owen looked at the Welsh Dragon. "I did no such thing! Nor did I kill Gruber. I'm no murderer. You have your murderer and you know it."

The tension drained from Owen. He placed both hands in his pocket and hung his head. "Mother, give Ferguson the clothes we both wore that day."

Mrs. Llewelyn stared at her son for a moment then turned and walked away.

John knew they were crazy if they hadn't washed the clothes or thrown them out, but their reactions had convinced him that he should be looking for evidence here. He needed to question Owen and knew it would be more effective enclosed in a room at the police station.

"I need you to come to the station, Owen, in a couple of hours, or I will send an officer to collect you."

"What for?"

"Your knife killed a man your beloved Anne and your mother hated."

Once Mrs. Llewelyn returned with a bag of clothes from the day of Gruber's murder, John tucked them under his arm and left the butcher's shop.

He returned to the station expecting to find Mullins and Lisle.

"Has DC Mullins checked in? Or Kitchen"

John had assigned Kitchen to go with Mullins, but neither man had checked in. He told the desk sergeant when to expect Owen Llewelyn and what to do if he didn't show up on his own. He asked to be taken to wherever the chief held David Gruber for questioning.

"Ah, Ferguson, David and I were just getting started. I asked him..."

John cut Weems off to disconcert Gruber and establish the interview, and himself, as especially important. "Why did you move to...where is it you live now? Winchester?"

David looked confused. "What difference does it..."

John raised his voice. "You moved far away from your father, had little contact with him these last two or three years, it seems, yet you feel slighted that he gave his money to people who cared about him here in York."

"Who says I had little contact?" David's face reddened and he fidgeted in his chair. He looked to Weems.

John repeated, "What made you move away from here, David?

"I wanted..." He started again, calmer. "My father and I didn't get along. I never did anything to please him. I worked in the pawnshop for years. I didn't like the work. After Mother died, we had nothing to say to each other. I moved to Winchester after that, found a good job. My family is happy. I merely assumed he would leave me everything when he died. I guess it shocked me to find out I meant so little to him. It shouldn't have, I suppose.

Weems resumed questioning. "David, he left you everything in the shop. That's not too bad an inheritance."

"I know, but it surprised me, that's all. It's not like I counted on his money or anything."

"Really? Where do you work?" John took over the questioning again.

"I work in a bank."

"A bank clerk.

That's not an awfully good job for a man around forty with a family, is it?"

David straightened and glared at John. "Actually, I'm the head cashier. I supervise ten or so other people."

John looked at Weems. His interest in the dead man's son rapidly deflated. He motioned Weems out of the interview room, into the hallway. "You finish up with him, Weems. We can check out his story about his job and happy life in Winchester later. I am going to check out some things that are bothering me." Something Anne said earlier disturbed him. Why hadn't he found the wet red jacket last night?

"Who found the jacket this morning?"

Weems looked around the station and pointed to a tall officer slouching near the front door drinking a mug of tea, nodding and speaking to two other constables as they left the building.

"Calvin Jones is his name." Weems watched John walk away, toward the constable, and considered whether any of their investigation so far had gotten them any closer to the truth.

Constable Jones stood to attention as the Scotland Yard man came up to him. "Constable Jones? John Ferguson." They shook hands. "I understand there were numerous spectators gathered around the front door as policemen searched Anne's chemist shop. Could you identify any of them?"

"Probably nearly all of them, sir."

"And were the Llewelyns there?"

"Uh, yes. At least the mother was."

"How about the doctor?"

The constable nodded.

"I need to know where exactly you found the red jacket in the chemist shop."

"Well, sir, I found it all balled up, you know, behind the front counter in the store."

"Had it been hidden? Perhaps a box or something thrown over it to hide it further?"

Eddie's solemn face peered into John's mind without warning.

"No, sir. I only went behind the counter and there it lay."

"Could you come and show me exactly where you found it? I think it might be important."

He imagined Eddie tugging on his pants. Trying so hard to make him understand something.

"Certainly, sir. Let me get the key from the sergeant in case the shop is locked. We checked that Lisle and little Eddie were safe and sound inside, then we secured our exit as we arrested Mrs. Winthrop."

John walked with Constable Jones down the block. He became more troubled. Something eluded him. Eddie's sad face, retreating from him over Lisle's shoulder yesterday.

The pair reached the front door of the chemist shop. It was locked.

"Maybe Lisle isn't in the mood to open up this morning." Jones turned the key in the lock and they entered. Sunlight lit the shop through the front windows. Only silence and the familiar herbal fragrance greeted them.

John called out as he pushed aside the curtain to the back rooms.

"Hello. Anyone here?" No sound. "Mullins, Lisle!" Silence. Mullins had not returned with Lisle and Eddie. He looked to Constable Jones who moved immediately behind the counter.

"Right here, sir. All rolled up and stuffed in here." Jones pointed to one of the low shelves. "Nothing sat in front of it. Quite easy to see."

"The thing is, I looked right where you are pointing last night. Granted I didn't do a thorough search, but from what you're showing me, I should have easily seen the coat."

Eddie's frustrated and disappointed face returned to John's mind.

"Yes, sir. Officers secured the shop from when Mrs. Winthrop got escorted back here from Dr. Berry's. No one came in here, sir."

"Were officers stationed in front and back?"

"No, sir. Only the one officer who checked the doors was locked and then stayed out back until we was ordered in to search this morning."

"He stood out there in the pouring rain in the blackness of the alley for hours? Just the one man?"

"Yes, sir. You can question him if you'd like." Jones thought a moment before speaking again, trying not to be disrespectful. "The front lock didn't look to be messed with, sir. The coat must have been hidden somewhere upstairs and moved early this morning by someone in the house."

John nodded trying to remember that word that Eddie kept saying? "Quack! That's it!"

"That's what, sir?"

"'Quack.' That's the word little Eddie kept saying to me. What does 'Quack' mean? Do you know little Eddie, Constable Jones?"

"A little. I know who he is."

"Well, he is a little boy who doesn't speak clearly. He kept trying to tell me something. What does quack sound like?"

"Well, it sounds like a duck. But he's talking about his mummy's accident, her crash—that's it. Crash. Quack. Crash."

"Of course it does! How could I have not understood? A crash? Like a car crash. Now I remember. 'Mummy goes quack.' That's what he said." John's excitement infected the officer.

"But his mummy wasn't in a car crash, his grandmother was."

"Yes, but Eddie wasn't with Anne and her mother when the accident occurred or the tailor would have known." John remembered. "Lisle calls Anne's mother '*mamie*' which is French for granny. Maybe Eddie does too. He spends a lot of time with Lisle. 'Granny went quack.'" He saw it. "Lisle had to have been there when the car hit Mrs. Thornton for him to have been there. Lisle denied that and Eddie tried to tell me the truth. Lisle pushed Mrs. Thornton? Is that possible? Why?"

The constable's expression told John that he had lost the thread of the explanation.

Pieces began falling into place for John. Lisle pushed Ruth Thornton's wheelchair into traffic and tried to kill her at Dr. Berry's when she thought *Mamie* might be able to tell them who pushed her. The red jacket belonged to Lisle which explains why Anne refused to talk and how it mysteriously appeared the next morning crumpled under the counter. Anne was protecting Lisle. Why would Lisle try to kill her grandmother? "I'm still missing something. Mullins is with her. Alone!"

"Sir?"

"Never mind. We need to get back to the station fast. And we need to find Kitchen and Mullins." John pivoted toward the door. "I saw DC Mullins with Lisle and Eddie leaving here an hour or so ago."

John and Constable Jones hurried back to the station. Jones stopped at the front desk to check on the whereabouts of the two police officers while John went directly downstairs to confront Anne. He yelled over his shoulder, "Get Weems."

Anne still sat on the cot staring at the wall, but she now had a blanket over her shoulders.

"Anne, I know you are protecting Lisle," he began, breathlessly.

Startled, she turned and looked at him.

"That jacket is hers. She attacked your mother and I know why. She pushed her wheelchair into traffic and tried to kill her. Lisle tried again last night to kill her at the doctor's office before your mother could tell us who pushed her into traffic."

Tears streaming down her face, she shook her head. "But what possible reason would she have for harming my mother?"

"She sees your mother as a threat to her for some reason."

"But that's absurd. How could she be?"

"Anne, I saw Lisle and Mullins and Eddie walking away from the shop an hour ago. Where did she lead them?"

Anne just shook her head.

"Has Lisle been hurting Eddie? Is that why he has so many accidents and has to be taken to Dr. Berry so often?"

Anne continued to shake her head. "No. That can't be true. Why? Why hurt Eddie?"

By the lack of conviction in her denial, John knew she had previously given the possibility some thought.

Weems, with Officer Jones following, clattered down the stairs.

"What's going on, Ferguson?"

John explained what he now suspected.

"I need you to release Anne. We need to find my officer and Lisle and Eddie. Soon! Mullins's questions may be threatening her, and I believe his life is in danger—maybe even Eddie's life."

More clattering down the stairs. Another young constable stuck his head around the stairs.

"Sir, Kitchen just rang the station. He's somewhere in Old Town. Says he's been following DC Mullins, nothing's happening, and wants to know if he should return to the station. He had to hang up but will ring again shortly."

Eddie walked between Lisle and Mullins, holding Mullins' hand. Lisle was silent.

Lisle had promised to show him something important, so Mullins let her lead, but he sensed they had been ambling around Old Town aimlessly. Then the shops along the street became familiar to him again and he recognized they were nearing the wrought iron gate which led back to the chapel. Where the pictures had been taken.

"Lisle, you need to talk to me."

Her long hair encircled her face, halo-like. She said nothing.

"Would you like a cup of tea, Lisle?"

Eddie perked up and looked at Lisle, hoping there might be a biscuit for him if they stopped.

It occurred to Mullins that he probably had the same look on his face, hoping Lisle would say yes.

She shook her head.

Mullins and Eddie looked at each other, disappointed.

They neared the gate and Mullins watched for recognition in Lisle's eyes, but she looked straight ahead as if that gateway meant nothing to her. She gazed down the cobblestone street full of busy people shopping and talking. It gave him the courage he needed.

He took a deep breath and said, "Lisle, we need to go through this gate, to the chapel behind it. You need to tell me about the photographs."

Lisle's face froze for half a second. Then, before Mullin's eyes, it changed to a purposeful expression. She had made a decision and nodded.

The wrought iron gate squeaked when he pushed it open. The cobblestone street led onto a flagstone path set in the narrow space between the old buildings and past the little abandoned church that Charlie Parker had taken him to. The pictures in his pocket of Lisle, posed naked on the altar, ran through his mind.

Lisle pushed open the peeling, once-white picket gate set in the lichen covered, stone fence that surrounded the weedy churchyard. She led them up to the church door, held it open inviting, or maybe daring, Mullins to come inside with her.

His heart skipped a beat. This was probably the first time she had directly looked at him. *Now we are getting somewhere,*" he thought, as he stepped past her into the gloom. Eddie followed him.

With a light touch, Lisle closed the door behind them. She slipped the knife from her purse concealing it behind her.

"Hello, I need to talk to Ferguson urgently! Bring him to the phone."

John rushed up the stairs. "Kitchen, where are you? Are you still following Mullins?"

"Yes sir. I believe Lisle is leading him somewhere. I followed them to Deangate Street, but I had to abandon my surveillance when I spotted a shop with a telephone."

"Don't interfere unless it's absolutely necessary. It could be very dangerous. I think Mullins might get her to open up. We'll be there as fast as we can."

Weems reluctantly allowed Anne out of the cell under their supervision. One of the two York police cars had been cranked into life and sent round to pick them up. Constable Jones clambered into the back seat next to Anne. Weems drove. John climbed in to his left. They sped off from the station toward Old Town.

They drove slowly down Deangate Street hoping to spot Kitchen.

John pulled the pictures of Lisle out of his pocket and handed them to Weems. "This is a church in Old Town. Do you recognize it?"

"Blimey! What is this?" He abruptly stopped the car. "Who took these? Is this Will's work?" Weems' jaw dropped and he kept staring.

"What is it? What are you looking at?" Anne said.

John asked Weems again, "Do you know this church?"

Weems shook his head while shuffling through the pictures.

"Let me see those." Anne reached forward. Weems glanced at John, who nodded in agreement. Weems handed the pictures back to Anne. Both men turned around to watch her reaction.

She paled and stared. Her face reflected sadness more than shock or anger.

Anne closed her eyes and held the pictures up to her chest to hide them.

"Does anyone know the location of this church in Old Town," John asked.

"May I see one of the pictures again. Maybe I can help," Weems said.

Anne reluctantly handed one photo to Jones.

"This is obviously an abandoned church."

Weems looked at the photo. "It looks rather small, more like a chapel from this shot."

John asked, "Can you help us find this, Anne. Eddie is with her."

She snapped at them. "Of course Eddie is with her. He is always with her. I wish I did know."

Jones said, "So many of these chapels have been built and abandoned over the centuries. It'd be near impossible to find without no other clues."

The other images taken by Will that were discovered in the chest in his room, including one of a walled churchyard, were still in John's possession. He dug it out of a pocket. John, Weems, Jones, and Anne all looked at the photo but no one recognized the altar or could say it was the same building.

"I guess we just go there and start asking around." Weems started the car moving again.

"Stop at The Swan. I have an idea who can help if we can find him," John said.

———

Mullins, Lisle, and Eddie stood in front of the stone altar where Will had taken the lewd photos. Mullins turned to see Eddie, who warily explored the little sanctuary, keeping near the walls. Eddie appeared unfamiliar with the place. The altar didn't interest him. Mullins concluded he probably hadn't been with Lisle when she was here with Will. At least he hoped that was true.

Lisle asked Mullins—the first thing she had said since they entered the church, "Has Anne seen these pictures?" She gripped the knife tighter awaiting his answer.

He shook his head. "No. Anne hasn't seen the photos. She really doesn't need to if you help us out." She came up behind him with such speed and force that he barely had time to turn his head before she was upon him.

———

The grass and weeds, wet from the recent rains, stuck to the sides and bottoms of Kitchen's boots and made a whisper with each step as he crept up to one of the windows near the door of the church. To see better through the old, crusted window, he wiped a clean spot with the sleeve of his shirt and peered into the gloom. He could see nothing. He looked around for something to stand on as the bottom edge of the windows along the sides began to rise higher above the ground. He found an old wooden box at the back, set it on the ground, and stood on top of it.

He peeked through the window. If the sun cast his shadow inside, he would be revealed outside. It shone in from the opposite side.

He rubbed another spot on the window. He had been told when he made his phone call that this was a dangerous situation and he should not make contact with Mullins. He couldn't understand what the danger might be.

Ah, he spotted them—Mullins, Lisle, and Eddie—from here. Diffused light streamed in through the tall windows on the other side. The threesome stood in front of the altar talking. Danger? *What could be dangerous about them?*

Then Lisle lunged. She pulled Mullins's head back by his hair. She slit his throat.

Mullins dropped to the floor, blood pooling, gushing down the front of him. She raised the knife to strike again, then halted and looked directly at Kitchen through the window.

Only then did he realize he was screaming and beating on the glass panes.

She turned, ran, and grabbed up Eddie with the other hand.

Kitchen fell backward off the box and scrambled to his feet. He didn't slow his pace although he had no weapon to use against her. He heard Eddie screaming as she flung open the door and ran for the gate. As he rounded the corner of the church, she opened the gate turning and brandishing the knife, first towards him then pointing it towards Eddie. Kitchen thought he might charge her and throttle her, knife or not, but knew that would only fail. People walking the path from Deangate Street, stopped to find the source of the screams.

Lisle could be hunted down later.

"Help! I need a doctor! Someone, Help!" Lisle ran, holding the terrified, shrieking Eddie in one arm and brandishing the bloody knife in the other. She forced Kitchen and the bystanders back. Her long blond hair flew out behind as she raced away from her latest bloody work. Kitchen turned and ran inside the church.

John and Weems had rounded up Will's brother, Charlie, who was squeezed in between the two police officers in the front seat. Charlie was leading them to the little Holy Trinity Church.

"Stop. Stop," Charlie commanded. He motioned John, Weems, and Jones out of the car and led them through the wrought iron gate. From there they could see a crowd gathering near the church gate. As they pushed through the crowd, John saw more people gaping through the door inside the church. He held his breath and ran inside. Once inside, he saw Patrick Mullins lying where he had dropped in a pool of his own blood. Strangers, and Kitchen, knelt over him.

Unable to comprehend how this could have happened, tears streamed down Kitchen's face. "He's dead. She's killed him. Slit his throat."

John's knees buckled and he sat in the dust on the cold stone floor. "No!" he screamed, the same scream he screamed as he watched his sergeant drop, headless, into a pool of his own blood. The same scream that had launched him into his own private hell. Yet, even after seeing Mullins' body, he was still here. Mentally. Physically. Reality wasn't leaving this time.

"Kitchen, where did she go?"

Anne's voice quivered. "Where is Eddie? Does she have him?"

John rose, knowing he had no time to think of the dead now. He had to find Eddie. Lisle might decide to kill him too.

Kitchen got up to follow.

"You stay with Mullins. Call for more officers and an ambulance," John ordered.

Kitchen's jaw shot out defiantly. "No, sir. I'm coming with you."

"But I need you here."

"Kitchen--" Weems added, hoping to dissuade Kitchen from following John

"No sir. I watched her do this. I'm coming to stop her. Fire me then, but I'm coming with you."

"I'll see to it. Maybe Kitchen can help. Go." Weems conceded.

John asked, "Where did she take the boy?"

Kitchen shook his head. "I didn't see where she went."

Jones stepped in and shouted toward John. "This way, sir. Some people out here saw her run off with the boy. She ran down Mad Alice Lane."

John rose and turned to Anne who was staring open-mouthed at Mullins's limp body.

"Anne, come with us. Maybe you can talk to her."

He held out his hand.

Anne grabbed it. Together, with Kitchen and Jones following, they ran outside, down the lane where people pointed.

John trotted past a miniature courtyard in the direction Jones had indicated, down Mad Alice Lane. They turned left at one of Old Town's larger streets, following stunned, horrified people pointing the way, then down Three Cranes Lane, a narrow funnel of tightly packed houses, well-trodden paving stones strewn with litter. Seeing no one down this narrow, dark lane, John slowed to a walk. He half held his breath listening, yet he heard only their own footsteps on the stones.

Then from the far end of the roadway, a young man stepped out, saw them, and shouted, "She's in the Three Cranes." He pointed at the side of a building.

John and the others hurried around to the front of a pub where a sign with a picture of three cranes in flight and large green letters spelling out the name, swung over the door in the damp cold. Several men stood near the bottom step of the pub's doorway and when John and his cohorts rounded the corner with Anne, the men in front of the door pointed inside without a word.

John rushed in ahead of the others, blinded at first in the dim room. He heard Eddie snuffling. As John's eyes adjusted, he saw a low, oak-beamed ceiling in the small room lined with dark oak paneling. A massive bar took nearly the whole length of the place, with room enough for only one row of small tables in front. The few people inside, as well as the bartender, remained silent as if a loud noise might frighten the girl into doing something horrible. A narrow staircase on the right led upstairs. Anne spotted her first.

Lisle sat on the third stair with Eddie on her knee. She held the knife to his squirming throat.

"Mummy!" Eddie cried and squirmed, hoping to release Lisle's grasp, but she held him tighter.

"Be still, Sweetie. Let Lisle hold you for now." Anne spoke to him calmly.

"Anne?" Lisle's voice was pleading.

John was about to touch Anne's back to caution her, but she spoke gently, with a tremulous voice to Lisle.

"What's going on, Lisle, darling?"

"I only meant to help you, Anne. I want you to be happy." Her eyes were glassy as she spoke.

"What do you mean? What did you do?"

"I've made all the people who made you sad go away. Mr. Gruber always made you so upset and angry. And now he won't. He can't hurt you or *Mamie* anymore. I pleaded with him, told him he had to leave you alone, but he wouldn't listen. He said I was crazy. He said he would tell you to send me away. I had to make him be quiet. And Will. Will took pictures of me like the soldiers did. He said he would protect me from other men touching me if I let him. I thought that would be good. Then when I refused to let him…do anything else to me he threatened to show the pictures to you. At the dance he made you so angry. I couldn't let him do that to you. I love you. You saved me from the soldiers. After the others left, I told him to meet me on the wall and I stopped him from ever making you unhappy again."

"But Lisle, why would you hurt your *mamie*? You know I love her."

"You said she made so much trouble and so much work. She made you cry. If I made her go away, you would be so much happier."

Anne started sobbing, barely able to speak. "Lisle, why have you been hurting Eddie?"

Lisle squirmed a little. She paused to think before answering.

Thinking she was distracted, both Kitchen and Jones eased a step towards her.

"Stop!" She pushed up to the fourth step, pulling Eddie with her. She stretched Eddie's neck, bringing the knife closer and tighter as he squirmed again.

"Eddie, stay still," Anne commanded him.

John motioned the two young men to back away from her.

"Lisle, why do you hurt Eddie? You know how much I love him."

Lisle was uneasy. "You love him more than me. I need you to love me. Don't you see? You have to understand. We don't need Eddie. We would be happier if he weren't around."

Anne was unsure what to say with the knife so close to Eddie's throat. She shook her head a little and stared at Lisle. "No, Lisle, we wouldn't be happier without him. We love him."

Lisle jumped up with her arm still around Eddie, stretching his neck again, cutting off his circulation.

"See you do love him more. Why? He never helps you. I help you all the time. He doesn't deserve your love. He's a bad boy."

As she said each of these last words, she tapped his head with the flat of the knife.

Anne gasped, "Don't hurt him."

Lisle raised the knife over Eddie's head in a stabbing position.

John lunged for her.

She dropped Eddie on the step and ran up the stairs followed closely by John, Kitchen, and Jones, while Anne snatched up the terrified little boy. Lisle ran through one of the upstairs rooms just ahead of John. He reached for her just before she threw herself through the glass of the window and plummeted to the street below.

John looked down where she had landed, her crumpled body, with the knife plunged into her chest. He turned away from another dead body and, still in reality, walked slowly down the stairs and out to the street where Anne had fallen on her knees in front of Lisle. She still clutched Eddie tightly.

"Why?" she asked Lisle's lifeless body.

Then she turned to John. "Why? I loved her so much. Why?"

He had no easy answers. Lisle's pain, like his, had come from the bloody war, he was sure. Looking around at all the faces staring in disbelief at the body of a beautiful young girl, John thought maybe the lingering pain of so many might etch itself into the collective memory.

Maybe the world will learn from the horror it had emerged from and there will never be another war.

Chapter 9

"Children, with eyes that hate you, broken and mad."

(November 17, 1920—Five days later—London)

With all of the ancient, carved tombs cramming Westminster Abbey in London, the anonymous grave of the Unknown Soldier immediately assumed precedence over all of them. Its pathos was irresistible. Not a family in all of Britain remained untouched by the years of slaughter. In the first five days after the Armistice ceremony, over a million people visited the grave and left a hundred thousand wreaths at the Cenotaph, which had become obscured by flowers. Every day at the Abbey, private items were laid at the tomb.

John stood in line outside the Abbey with hundreds of others, slowly working their way up to file past the grave. Few people even spoke as they inched forward, lost in their own thoughts. He had just gotten off the train in London from York. The cabbie dropped him at the end of the line which stretched two long blocks from the Abbey. The wind forced him to turn up the collar of his heavy raincoat. Cars appeared out of the dense fog and chugged past, splashing water as they bumped through dips. A wagon loaded with kegs of ale pulled by four matching, dappled, white Irish draft horses, passed him. It pleased him to watch these horses that had been used exten-sively during the war to pull artillery through the mud. So many of them had perished during the war, they were near extinct, yet here they were, proudly pulling their load.

Clutching his suitcase filled with his case notes, John shuffled forward with the others as the line moved ahead. He reflected on the York investiga-tion, his first important case since the end of the war.

The day in Old Town he had waited with Anne, Eddie in her arms, while police swarmed around Lisle's body. Eventually, he asked one of the consta-bles if Patrick had been taken to the morgue in the basement of the hospital.

The surprised young man nodded. "Yes, sir. He's been taken to hospital. But, sir, he ain't dead."

John choked up even now, five days later in London, queuing to see the Unknown Soldier. *But, sir, he ain't dead.* More wonderful words, he could not imagine.

John had learned that, by sheer luck, a doctor on the street that day heard Kitchen scream and rushed over to help Mullins. The knife Lisle had taken was not very sharp—just as Anne had pointed out to him that day in her shop. And although Patrick lost a lot of blood, it had not sliced his carotid artery. The doctor had stanched the flow of blood, and an ambulance had been summoned even before John had seen him lying there. If he hadn't run out of the chapel so fast, he would have learned the man who bent over Patrick's body was a doctor. The sight of Patrick's body lying on the stone floor had struck him so disturbingly, like Sergeant Tipper, that even now a cold shiver ran through him.

But, sir, he ain't dead. Beautiful words indeed.

He had left Mullins in Dr. Berry's good care before he left for London this morning. Mullins looked pale, but he sat up, sipping some liquid through a straw.

From his place in line, John pictured Mullins being pampered and anxious to return to London and work. He will be coming home in a few days.

He wanted to see Anne one last time before he left for London. He found her smiling at her mother, Eddie in her arms. Mrs. Thornton gestured animatedly and flashed a crooked smile toward John as he entered. Owen stood with his arm around both Anne and Eddie. When Anne looked up and saw John, the contented look on her face told him that she was in the right place with the right people. He still couldn't say exactly what about her had given him strength, but he was thankful to her for that.

Kitchen drove John to the train station and asked him to keep an eye open for a job for him in London with Scotland Yard. John assured him he would.

His thoughts raced back to the present as he passed through the west door of the Abbey and saw the Tomb of the Unknown Warrior. He stepped next to it and saw the marble slab upon which single flowers, rosaries, and small private things of all kinds had been dropped, including a United States Congressional Medal. He had nothing to lay on it. Tears silently rolled down his cheeks.

He shuffled on with the other mourners, each clutching their own losses, perhaps eased by the dignity and magnificence of this unknown man's burial and funeral ceremony.

John stepped from the hush of the Abbey, back onto the street, and inhaled deeply the wintry November air, air as fresh as it gets in London. The rain stopped and the fog slowly lifted but the icy wind pushed at him as he walked on to Scotland Yard, pulling up the collar of his overcoat once again and planting his feet firmly within reality. He adjusted his suitcase and thought about all the survivors.

Survivors

No doubt they'll soon get well; the shock and strain

Have caused their stammering, disconnected talk.

Of course they're "longing to go out again," —

These boys with old, scared faces, learning to walk.

They'll soon forget their haunted nights; their cowed

Subjection to the ghosts of friends who died, —

Their dreams that drip with murder; and they'll be proud

Of glorious war that shatter'd all their pride.

Men who went out to battle, grim and glad;

Children, with eyes that hate you, broken and mad.

"Survivors" was written by Siegfried Sassoon (1886–1967), a young Englishman who said goodbye to his idealistic life and rode off on his bicycle to join the Army and fought in WWI. He wrote this while in the mental institution Craiglockart in Scotland in 1917.

SOURCES
"Survivors," by Siegfried Sassoon (1886-1967). The Harry Ransom Center / The Siegfried Sassoon Literary Estate via *First World War Poetry Digital Archive*, accessed October 12, 2022, http://ww1lit.nsms.ox.ac.uk/ww1lit/collections/item/9686.813

ABOUT THE AUTHOR

Vicki Kinzie is an American novelist, an experienced traveler, an avid mystery reader, and history devotee and teacher of twenty years. Vicki puts her knowledge and passions together to take her readers on adventures through murder and mazes across ancient streets and times. She loves to travel and spent several summers sailing around northern Europe, including much of England with her husband. Vicki lives in Colorado with her husband and dogs.

www.ingramcontent.com/pod-product-compliance
Lightning Source LLC
Chambersburg PA
CBHW060454300726
48975CB00008B/2516